Rose & Other Stories

Edited by Sarah Dahlmann

Mantler Publishing

CONTENTS

ROSE

Seraton:
Developed in 1994 by government scientists, it was supposed to wipe the memories of government spies and secret service agents who were captured in an effort prevent loss of confidential information through torture. The memory loss wore off with discontinued use. However, the trials showed the drug caused a violent reaction when initially given. To stop this, a sedative was added. The sedative mixed with the drug made the test subjects semi-catatonic. In 1996, the funding for the research was cut and the drug declared useless. The patent for the drug was bought by a private company in 1997.

June 5, 2006

The nurse at the front desk looked up as the woman was brought in by a man wearing a long leather jacket and blue jeans. His brown hair was done in a military haircut and his blue eyes looked tired. The woman was wearing an overcoat, her brown hair hung in her face and her arms crossed over her chest.

"Can I help you?" The nurse asked, looking at the woman. The woman's eyes peered out from under the hair.

"I'm looking for Dr. Fenton," The man said, "I talked to him on the phone yesterday."

"Have seat and I will call him for you," The nurse said.

"Thank you," The man said. He turned and directed the woman to the nearby couch. There weren't many people in the waiting area, so there was lots of space to sit down. The nurse watched them sit down before turning away to pick up the phone. She had dialed the first two digits of the extension when there was a ruckus at the door. She looked up to see two police officers fighting to bring an escaped patient back into the building. The nurse put the phone down and ran to get some orderlies to help out the police officers.

The waiting room got busy for several minutes as the orderlies arrived and the patient was sedated. The patient was dragged away and the police left. The waiting area was quiet once again and the nurse sat down at her station. She picked up the phone and dialed Dr. Fenton's extension. She informed him that a man and woman were waiting for him and that the man had phoned him the day before. Dr. Fenton said he would be right down.

The nurse glanced over at the couch. The woman was curled up in a ball against the arm of the couch, but the man was no longer sitting beside her. The nurse looked around the waiting area, but the man was nowhere in sight. The nurse stood up, went around the desk, and approached the woman.

"Where did he go?" The nurse asked. The woman shrugged.

"He said that he would be back," The woman's voice was muffled, "And I should wait for him."

The nurse saw a piece of paper beside the woman and picked it up. It was an admission paper, but the only thing filled out was the signature of the person who could sign her out and that was unreadable. The spaces for name, birthday, and everything else were blank.

"Nurse?" Dr. Fenton asked from behind her. The nurse turned to him.

"This is the woman," The nurse said, "But the man disappeared. He just left this." The nurse offered the paper. Dr. Fenton took it and looked it over.

"Well, let's get her in for an evaluation." Dr. Fenton said, "Perhaps she can fill in these blanks."

"All right," The nurse said. She headed back to her desk to gather the rest of the paperwork Dr. Fenton would need.

Dr. Fenton stepped closer to the woman. She peered up at him.

"Miss," Dr. Fenton said, "Will you please come with me?"

"He'll be back," The woman answered, "I am supposed to wait for him."

"Why don't you come and wait inside?" Dr. Fenton asked, "It's more comfortable." Dr. Fenton took the woman's arm and tried to get her to stand up.

"No!" The woman screamed and scratched Dr. Fenton to get him to let go of her. Dr. Fenton pulled his arm back. The scratches were deep enough that the cuts welled up with blood.

Dr. Fenton could hear the nurse call for the orderlies. The woman kept Dr. Fenton at a distance by scratching at him if he tried to touch her. The orderlies arrived and each took an arm as they pulled her off the couch. She started screaming again and repeated that the man was coming back and she was supposed to wait for him. She fought as the orderlies dragged her through the doors and into the hospital itself. Dr. Fenton followed them as he pressed the cuts with the sleeve of his shirt.

They got the woman sedated before putting her in a padded room. She slumped down in the corner where the orderlies set her. The orderlies left, but Dr. Fenton stayed a minute more. He crouched down beside her.

"I'll take care of you, Rose, just like you asked me to." He patted the woman's shoulder before straightening up and leaving the room.

May 7, 2012

Dr. Fenton stood at the window of his office, watching the patients wander the grounds. The ones that were allowed out were dressed in coats appropriate for the weather, but it made them a little harder to tell apart. If he hadn't been head doctor of the hospital for so many years and knew all the patients as well as he did, he would have had more trouble. However, each of them stood or sat in their usual places in the grounds.

Rose was by the rose bushes. She was checking on them. The gardener was supposed to be the person who took care of the flowers on the grounds, but even he would be the first to say that it was Rose who took care of them. One of the nurses had asked for roses to be planted on the grounds in memory of her husband, who had a mental breakdown and jumped off the roof. The gardener had done it. He didn't think they would last because he didn't know much about growing roses, but then Rose arrived. She might not talk much, or at all most days, but she had instructed the gardener how to take care of the roses. The gardener might have just handed over his tools to Rose and let her go, but Dr. Fenton had expressed concern about giving Rose sharp implements.

The phone rang. Dr. Fenton turned from the window to pick it up.

"Yes?"

"Dr. Radburn is here to see you," The nurse at the front desk said.

"Have him escorted up," Dr. Fenton said.

"Yes, Doctor," The nurse said. Dr. Fenton put the phone back before turning to the window. The patients wandered around the grounds lost in their own realities, completely unaware of what was going on anywhere else. If he didn't know what their realities were like, Dr. Fenton might envy them. After all no one had told them what was going on.

A member of the board had realized that Dr. Fenton had been the doctor at the mental hospital for thirty years, which meant that they felt it was time for him to retire his position. This Dr. Radburn was supposed to be his replacement. The switch was supposed to be immediate, but then it was decided that Dr. Fenton would mentor Dr. Radburn. Dr. Fenton knew that it was the better idea, but still felt like he was being pushed aside for the newer and supposedly better. Not that they were asking him to leave at the end of the six months, but he would take a backseat to Dr. Radburn. Dr. Fenton had spent some time counting his savings to see if he could retire yet, but found it a little bit short of his goal. He hoped that he could find another job or another source of income before the six months were up.

There was a knock at the door.

"Come in," Dr. Fenton called. He heard the door open and someone come in. The person stopped and the door was closed. Dr. Fenton looked over his shoulder to study the man. The man was average height and looked in good shape for a doctor. His arms, chest, shoulders, and even ankles were muscular. He had a jaw line that suggested an average man. His brown hair was neatly parted with a slight shine to it. Under a tan coat, he wore brown loafers, grey slacks that came just above his ankles, and a white dress shirt. His grey eyes scanned the room. He didn't appear to have any lips and his nose had been broken at least three times. To Dr. Fenton he looked more like body builder or a thug than a doctor.

"Dr. Radburn, I assume," Dr. Fenton said as he turned back to the window.

"Yes," Dr. Radburn replied, "You did get the notice about mentoring me."

"I did," Dr. Fenton said, "I was wondering where you had last worked."

"Is it relevant to anything in particular?" Dr. Radburn asked.

"I need to know what level of activity you are used to," Dr. Fenton asked, "So that I know where you can start."

"I can keep up with you," Dr. Radburn said, "It shouldn't be any trouble."

Down below on the grounds, Henry and Curtis had started fighting again. They were probably fighting about the chess game from three years ago. Dr. Fenton felt the pressure behind his eye that suggested the headache that went with a long night.

"We'll see," Dr. Fenton said as he turned from the

window. Dr. Radburn didn't respond or show any emotion.

"Let's start with a tour of the place," Dr. Fenton said as he walked passed Dr. Radburn toward the door.

Dr. Radburn didn't move. "I was told to come here to meet you and get my schedule. I was told that everything else would be left until tomorrow."

"I was told that being a doctor meant that there was plenty of time for golfing," Dr. Fenton responded, "But I haven't been able to do more than drive by a course in thirty-five years. Come on." Dr. Fenton opened the door and stepped into the hallway. He waited with the door open for two minutes before Dr. Radburn followed him out of the room. Dr. Fenton closed the door before heading off down the hallway.

Dr. Fenton pointed to things and identified them as he walked passed. He didn't look to see if Dr. Radburn was following him. They went through the fourth floor, which was administration and offices. It had once been for patients, but it was only floor with a ledge outside the windows and no bars on the windows, so it was changed to office space. The fifth floor, which led to the roof, was storage, so Dr. Fenton went down. In the middle of the hallway on the second floor they encountered the fight that had been brought inside with Henry and Curtis.

Dr. Fenton tried to separate the two patients by getting between them and getting them at arm's length. Dr. Radburn tried to grab Curtis from behind and pulled him away from Henry. Henry backed off, but Curtis started to struggle. Dr. Radburn tried to keep a grip on him, but Curtis got his arm free and smashed his elbow into Dr. Radburn's mouth. An orderly came down the hallway with a sedative. Dr. Fenton took the syringe while the orderly helped hold Curtis down. The needle went into

Curtis and quickly Curtis went limp. The orderly took Curtis to his room.

Once Dr. Radburn had finished icing his lip, Dr. Fenton finished the tour of the second floor and then the first floor. The tour ended at the front desk.

"Well, thank you for showing me around," Dr. Radburn said as he started to turn toward the exit.

"Come on," Dr. Fenton said cheerfully, "Since you are here, we should get you started. The best way to get acquainted is to help out with the distribution of medication." Dr. Fenton guided Dr. Radburn back into the ward.

Dr. Radburn was just short of swearing at Dr. Fenton as he stood over the nurse as she passed out the little cups of pills and water to the patients as they walked passed in a line up. He wasn't supposed to start until tomorrow, but Dr. Fenton hadn't paid any attention to the several times that Dr. Radburn had mentioned it. He had other places he needed to be at this moment. All the patients were on some sort of pill in this place. The nurse was carefully making sure that each patient got the cup for them and not any other cup. It was almost like she took pride in the level of organization that was put into all of this. Dr. Radburn didn't understand why anyone would have pride in something like that. It really wouldn't matter if patient medication got mixed up, as far as he could tell. They all looked to get the same amount of the same pill.

Dr. Radburn had watched the patients for a while too, but that got boring quickly. They all seemed to be about the same. All of them had mental problems and all of them shuffled along in a quiet and orderly fashion. Not one of them stuck out as being unusual. Slowly the line went passed. Each patient was handed the two cups. They put the pills in their mouths and then swallowed with the water. Then an orderly would take the cups and the patient would go back to whatever they were doing before it was time for medication.

Dr. Radburn knew that he would have to go through this every day for six months as well as individual sessions with some patients, but he wasn't supposed to start all this until tomorrow. Dr, Radburn was sure that he would have no problems keeping up, despite what Dr. Fenton thought. Dr. Radburn's attention was brought back to the patients.

A patient came down the line. She was five feet six inches and about a hundred and fifteen pounds by his guess, with brown hair that fell around her face. Her blues eyes appeared to be unfocused. And she wore the white clothes of a patient who didn't have anything else to wear. She shuffled slowly down the line without any apparent thoughts about what was going on. Dr. Radburn recognized her from the picture he had seen. His boss had tacked the picture up several years ago and it still hung on the wall. The picture had been put up as congratulations for being the best agent in the department, but had turned into a wanted poster after she had disappeared. Her name was Mina Tate. No one had seen or heard from her in years and here she was, a patient in line for medication in a mental hospital that the department wanted to take over so that they could keep prisoners there. Dr. Radburn's boss was going to be surprised when Dr. Radburn brought him that news. That was if Dr. Fenton would let Dr. Radburn out to check in with his boss.

"Hello, Rose," The nurse said to Mina, "Here is your medication for today. Dr. Fenton has you booked for an appointment as soon as you are finished here." Mina nodded. The nurse offered Mina the two cups. Mina took them and put the pill in her mouth before drinking the water. She handed the two cups to the orderly before walking away. She was headed to the area where Dr. Fenton held his therapy sessions. Dr. Radburn would have loved to be in that session, but knew he couldn't get into them until Dr. Fenton let him.

The next patient stepped up and Dr. Radburn had to go back to watching patients take their medication.

Dr. Fenton was sitting at the table with a file open in front of him when the door opened. Rose shuffled in and sat down in the chair opposite him. She looked at him and he looked back.

"How much to do you remember of your life before the mental hospital?" Dr. Fenton asked.

Rose shook her head.

"I know," Dr. Fenton said, "You don't remember what I told you last week, let alone a month ago." Rose nodded.

"But I need to talk this out to someone," Dr. Fenton said.

Rose was still.

"We have a new doctor coming in," Dr. Fenton said, "You saw him. I put him there watching the patients get medication. He expects me to follow whatever schedule was given to him, but I was told he would be starting today, so I had him start today. I will have to get out of here in time to prevent him from leaving after he has helped with the clean-up. But every time I look at him, I don't see a doctor. His file looks like a doctor's, but he himself doesn't. When you came to me with your plan six years ago, I thought you needed to be locked up when you started talking about spies and departments run by secret government organizations. I didn't understand why you were telling me so much, but now I do. You need me to protect you against whatever he wants to do with you. I don't know whether he is here to harm you or try to get you out, but our deal still stands and I will protect you from him."

Rose stared at Dr. Fenton blankly.

"You'll understand some day," Dr. Fenton patted her hand. "For now, just enjoy your roses."

Rose smiled at the mention of the flowers. Dr. Fenton patted her hand again and smiled back.

Dr. Radburn helped with the clean up after the handing out of the medication. When that was finished, Dr. Fenton came out of his session with Mina. Mina wandered off like all the patients, shuffling and looking lost.

Dr. Radburn went to Dr. Fenton to tell him that he was leaving, but he was also wondering about Mina.

"Finished with the medication?" Dr. Fenton asked.

"Yes," Dr. Radburn answered, "I was just wondering about-"

"Good, good," Dr. Fenton spoke over the second part, "Then you can join me in checking on our more severe cases."

"I'm not quite prepared," Dr. Radburn started.

"Very few people are," Dr. Fenton replied as he walked away. Dr. Radburn had to run to follow.

"What I mean-" Dr. Radburn started again.

"These cases are our most interesting cases," Dr. Fenton said, "But you also have to be careful with them. We try to keep them calm, but they do lash out." Dr. Fenton kept talking as he continued down the hallway and Dr. Radburn couldn't get a word in.

They reached the area for the dangerous patients. An orderly stood like a guard at the entry to the area. He let them through and followed them inside. Dr. Fenton stopped at the first door.

"In here is Raymond," Dr. Fenton said, "He is paranoid that everyone is out to kill him. He gets sedated regularly, but due to adverse reactions we can't get him on a regular medication schedule." Dr. Fenton opened the door and the two of them stepped inside. The orderly stayed in the doorway.

Raymond sat in the corner, looking at them like they were going to pull a weapon on him at any moment. He was in a straitjacket and yet looked comfortable that way.

"Hello, Raymond," Dr. Fenton said.

"Hello, Dr. Fenton," Raymond replied. "How are you?"

"I have a headache," Dr. Fenton answered, "I am here to introduce you to Dr. Radburn. He is the new doctor here."

"He is going to kill me," Raymond said when he looked toward Dr. Radburn.

"No, he isn't going to kill you," Dr. Fenton said, "He is the new doctor. He will take over your care."

"He'll kill me," Raymond yelled as he kicked himself into the corner. Dr. Fenton turned to Dr. Radburn and nodded the suggestion that he leave. Dr. Radburn moved back and the orderly let him leave.

"We'll try again another time," Dr. Fenton said. Raymond calmed down.

"Rest," Dr. Fenton told Raymond before leaving the room. The orderly closed the door.

"Some of our patients are like that," Dr. Fenton said, "Next time Raymond will meet you with less fear." They moved on to the next room.

"I see," Dr. Radburn said.

"This is Amber," Dr. Fenton said, "She is very unpredictable and medications have just made things worse." Dr. Fenton opened the door, but didn't enter. Sitting in the middle of the padded room was a woman in her early twenties. She would have been beautiful if there weren't a circle of feces around where she was sitting in the middle of the room. She didn't move, but turned to them and smiled.

"Good morning, Dr. Fenton," Amber said, "Who is the cute guy with you?"

"This is Dr. Radburn," Dr. Fenton said, "He is the new doctor."

"Come on in, Dr. Radburn," Amber invited with a flirty smile.

"We are introducing Dr. Radburn to all your neighbours," Dr. Fenton said, "So he can't visit at the moment. Perhaps another time."

"I'm here anytime you want," Amber smiled at Dr. Radburn. Dr. Fenton closed the door. A shudder went through Dr. Radburn.

"She'll give it up if you don't encourage it," Dr. Fenton said.

"And it will be uncomfortable until then," The orderly added with amusement. Dr. Radburn looked at the orderly, but found the man's face impassive. Dr. Fenton moved to the next door and Dr. Radburn had to catch up.

"This is Johnny," Dr. Fenton said, "Because we don't know his name, but John is much too formal for the boy."

"If he is a boy, why is he in this part of the mental hospital?" Dr. Radburn asked.

"Because none of the medication works on him," Dr. Fenton answered, "When he gets worked up the only thing we can do is to restrain him and calm him. So, do not excite him. To calm him, we sing a lullaby, usually until he is asleep because otherwise he will start getting excited again."

"Okay," Dr. Radburn said. Dr. Fenton opened the door and Dr. Radburn followed him inside.

Johnny was sitting against the wall and he looked up at them. He smiled at Dr. Fenton, but frowned at Dr. Radburn.

"Hello, Johnny," Dr. Fenton said, "I am here to introduce you to Dr. Radburn. He is the new doctor."

Johnny looked Dr. Radburn over, but didn't say anything.

"Hello, Johnny," Dr. Radburn said, trying to replicate Dr. Fenton's calm voice, "How are you today?"

Johnny looked like he was trying to remember Dr. Radburn's face. He squinted his eyes and pressed his lips together.

"Dr. Radburn is going to take over your care," Dr. Fenton said.

Johnny looked at Dr. Fenton and shook his head.

"It is okay," Dr. Fenton said, "Dr. Radburn is a good man." Dr. Fenton glanced at Dr. Radburn. "Offer to shake his hand."

Dr. Radburn hesitated a second before offering his hand to Johnny to shake. Johnny grabbed and held on for dear life. Dr. Radburn made noise that he was in pain.

"Johnny, we have talked about this," Dr. Fenton said, "Be gentle with people."

Rather than let up, Johnny clutched Dr. Radburn's hand tighter and started yelling.

"I'm sorry about that," Dr. Fenton said to Dr. Radburn, "We've been working on that and I thought he was getting better."

"What do I do now?" Dr. Radburn asked as he tried to

extract his hand without hurting Johnny.

"Sing," Dr. Fenton answered, "Until he falls asleep."

Dr. Radburn didn't look happy and was closer to hurting Johnny than singing.

"He'll let go if you sing," Dr. Fenton said, "He may not if I sing."

Dr. Radburn was not happy about it, but he started to sing a lullaby. He started quietly and very unsure about himself, but got louder as he went along. Johnny didn't loosen his grip, but he quit yelling. That gave Dr. Radburn enough to keep singing.

Dr. Fenton slowly moved back out of the room. Dr. Radburn was so focused on Johnny and singing that he didn't notice when the orderly quietly closed the door.

"How long do you think it will take Dr. Radburn to sing Johnny to sleep?" Dr. Fenton asked the orderly.

"Johnny woke up from his last nap only half an hour ago," The orderly answered, "It will likely take several hours before Dr. Radburn will be able to extract himself."

"Let him out and send him up to me when he does," Dr. Fenton said.

"Will do," The orderly replied. As Dr. Fenton headed out of the ward he could hear the orderly chuckling. Dr. Fenton didn't suppress his own smile.

May 8, 2012

Dr. Fenton arrived at the mental hospital rested and ready to face another day. He greeted the nurse at the reception desk before going passed her into the break room. As he was taking off his coat and putting it away, he noticed that Dr. Radburn's coat was still hanging up where he had left it.

Dr. Fenton finished putting his stuff away before going back out to the reception desk.

"Did Dr. Radburn go home yesterday?" Dr. Fenton asked. The nurse checked the records.

"If he did, he didn't stop to sign out," The nurse answered.

"Thank you," Dr. Fenton said. He headed for the area with the dangerous patients. The orderly opened the door for him and followed him down the hall to Johnny's room. Dr. Fenton looked in the window.

Dr. Radburn was leaning against the wall with his head fallen to his chest. Johnny was curled up beside him.

"Shall I get ready?" The orderly asked.

"No," Dr. Fenton replied, "Just let him out when he wakes up."

"I will," The orderly said.

Dr. Fenton left the ward and went up to his office. He had other work to do as well as making up Dr. Radburn's schedule. He had to make sure that Dr. Radburn was constantly busy from the time he arrived to the time he left and it all had to be away from the offices where the files were.

Dr. Radburn woke up to find Johnny crouched near him. But Johnny's eyes were unfocused and he was singing to himself. Dr. Radburn slowly got to his feet. He tried to avoid any jerky movement or anything that would startle Johnny. Then Dr. Radburn slowly made his way to the door of the room. He knocked lightly on the door. Johnny didn't seem to be aware of Dr. Radburn. Minutes went by before the door opened. The orderly held it open and Dr. Radburn stepped out. The orderly closed the door before heading back down the hallway. Dr. Radburn followed him.

"What time is it?" Dr. Radburn asked.

"Four o'clock," The orderly answered.

"In the morning?" Dr. Radburn asked.

"The afternoon, actually," The orderly answered.

"Why wasn't I woken up?" Dr. Radburn asked.

"You didn't ask to be," The orderly replied.

"From now on, I would like to be woken up if I fall asleep in there," Dr. Radburn said.

"I will make a note of that," The orderly said, "Dr. Fenton had said yesterday that he wanted to see you when you were finished. I don't know if he still wants to see you, but I would recommend you check in with him.

"Thank you for passing along the message," Dr. Radburn said.

They reached the end of the hallway and the orderly opened the door to let Dr. Radburn out. The doctor left and headed for the break room.

Dr. Radburn got a sandwich out of the machine and ate it before heading up to Dr. Fenton's office. Dr. Fenton was standing at the window when Dr. Radburn knocked on the door. Dr. Fenton turned around to see who it was.

"So, you finally decided to show up," Dr. Fenton said.

Dr. Radburn opened his mouth to defend himself, but realized how bad it would sound and closed his mouth.

"I put your schedule together," Dr. Fenton said, moving to his desk. He picked up a piece of paper and offered it to Dr. Radburn. Dr. Radburn stepped forward to take the piece of paper. He looked it over.

"Since you said that you could keep up, I assumed that you were being truthful," Dr. Fenton said, "If you find yourself having trouble, come talk to me. And make sure you are on time from now on."

"I will," Dr. Radburn said before leaving the office. He checked what he was supposed to be doing and went off to do that.

It was six thirty before Dr. Radburn had finished everything and was able to leave. The only thing that made Dr. Radburn feel better about it was the fact that Dr. Fenton was still there and likely to be there for a while.

Dr. Radburn headed back to the apartment that had been set up for him. He ignored the call of his stomach and the light from the answering machine. He went straight to his computer. He turned it on and went into the chat program. It took a minute before the other person came on.

"Where the hell were you?" Mr. Masters demanded, "You were supposed to call as soon as you got back from checking in with Dr. Fenton."

"I just got back from my first visit," Dr. Radburn answered, "He decided that I needed to be put to work immediately. Then he introduced me to some of the dangerous patents and I ended up singing one of them to sleep, which put me to sleep. I didn't wake up until four this afternoon, when he handed me my schedule and told me to get to work."

"Do you think he suspects anything?" Mr. Masters asked.

"I think he doesn't want to give up his position," Dr. Radburn answered.

"What is your schedule?" Mr. Masters asked.

"Eight to five Monday to Saturday with the possibility of more hours," Dr. Radburn answered.

"Is there anything else?" Mr. Masters asked.

"Mina Tate is a patient there," Dr. Radburn answered, "I saw her. She is catatonic, but it shouldn't be too hard to snap her out of it. She will need extensive retraining if you want her back."

"We want her back," Mr. Masters said, "Get a copy of

her file for us and we'll figure out what it will take."

"I will," Dr. Radburn said.

"Report in on Sunday," Mr. Masters said.

"I will," Dr. Radburn replied. Mr. Masters terminated the connection.

Dr. Fenton kept an eye on Dr. Radburn for the next several weeks. He watched as Dr. Radburn tried to find reasons to get at patient files and be allowed into therapy sessions. He watched as Dr. Radburn tried to avoid as much work as possible because doing everything asked of him was tiring and more than he was used to. Dr. Fenton did nothing to help Dr. Radburn and Dr. Radburn didn't come to him for help.

June 11, 2012

It was a month into being there that Dr. Radburn was helping get the medication ready. The nurse, Maureen, was pointing out the various pills and what they were. She took down one bottle without telling what it was and put one pill into a cup with a number beside it before putting the bottle back.

"What is that one?" Dr. Radburn asked.

"That is Rose's medication, Seraton" The nurse answered, "It is a sedative and it looks like it is running out." The nurse made a note on her pad before reaching for the next bottle of pills. She went back to what she had been doing. Dr. Radburn had no choice but to move on, even if he wanted to investigate. Any other questions would seem suspicious.

Dr. Fenton was gathering everything he needed for his next therapy session when there came a knock on the door. He wondered if it was Dr. Radburn again with another inane question.

"Come," Dr. Fenton kept the irritation out of his voice. The door opened and the nurse in charge of the medication stepped into the office.

"Yes?' Dr. Fenton's annoyance melted away.

"We are running out of Rose's medication," Maureen said.

"Send an order to inventory to get some more," Dr. Fenton said.

"Okay," Maureen said before turning and leaving the office. Dr. Fenton finished gathering everything he needed before leaving.

It was five in the evening when there came another knock on Dr. Fenton's door. This time he knew it wasn't Dr. Radburn to ask questions. Dr. Radburn had gone home half an hour ago after getting upset at Dr. Fenton for not being invited to join the therapy sessions.

"Come in," Dr. Fenton called. The door opened and the accountant, James, stepped into the office. He closed the door behind him before stepping up to the desk.

"I need to discuss a request I received this afternoon," James said, holding up the file he was carrying.

"Okay," Dr. Fenton said as he put down his pen and gave James his full attention.

"Inventory sent me a request to purchase more medication for Rose," James said.

"I am aware of that request," Dr. Fenton said, "Maureen brought it to me and I said to send the request to inventory. What is the problem with it?"

"The fund that was set up for Rose is running low," James answered, "There is enough for food and other such for the next month, but not enough for anything else. I checked with Maureen and she said that there is about three weeks of medication left. What would you like me to do?"

"Give me a few days to think about it," Dr. Fenton said, "I'll figure it out and get back to you."

"Very well," James said, "The request will sit on my desk until you have made your decision."

Dr. Fenton nodded and James left the office. Once the door closed, Dr. Fenton went back to his work. He worked for fifteen more minutes before giving up for the moment. He got up and left his office. Dr. Fenton went down to where the patient rooms were. No one disturbed him as he went along the hallway. He reached Rose's room and stopped to look in the window. Rose was lying on her bed with her eyes closed. She was likely to have just gotten to sleep.

Dr. Fenton left her alone and headed back to his office. She probably didn't remember enough to help him anyway.

June 14, 2012

Dr. Fenton had the files he needed set out on the table in the therapy room and was reviewing the notes from his last therapy session when there was a knock on the door. He glanced at his watch. It was too early for it to be his next appointment.

"Yes?" Dr. Fenton called. The door opened and Maureen was standing there.

"Dr. Radburn is making a nuisance of himself," Maureen said, "What should I do?"

"Send him in here," Dr. Fenton answered, "I will keep him out of your hair."

"Thank you," Maureen said. She left the door open when she headed out. Dr. Fenton straightened the stack of files, but otherwise stayed where he was.

Two minutes later, Dr. Radburn arrived and entered the room.

"You asked to see me," Dr. Radburn said.

"Yes," Dr. Fenton replied, "You are making a nuisance of yourself and that is making everyone else's job harder. I am sure you have other things to do with your time."

"I am just trying to do the jobs that you gave me," Dr. Radburn said.

"Then sit on the chair against the far wall and keep your mouth shut," Dr. Fenton said, "If you speak, you will find yourself cleaning up after the severe cases for a month."

Dr. Radburn winced at the threat before going and sitting down in the chair already set up. Dr. Fenton went back to reading through his notes.

It was half an hour later that there was a timid knock at the door. Dr. Fenton looked up to see Rose in the doorway.

"Come in," Dr. Fenton said. Rose stepped into the room and went to the chair on the other side of the table from Dr. Fenton. She sat down in the chair and set her hands on the table. Then she realized that they were shaking, so she moved them to her lap. Her eyes were much clearer than normal and she looked at Dr. Fenton's face rather than her hands or the table.

"How are you today?" Dr. Fenton asked.

Rose shrugged.

"How are the roses?" Dr. Fenton asked.

Rose smiled briefly then it disappeared.

"Are you taking your medication as you are supposed to?" Dr. Fenton asked.

Rose shook her head as she looked down at her hands.

"You need to take your medication," Dr. Fenton said, "Without it you end up back in a padded room and you don't like that. You don't like what happens when you don't take your medication. Will you go back on it?"

Rose nodded.

"Good," Dr. Fenton said, "Is there anything you would like to talk about?"

Rose shook her head.

"Then we'll talk again in a couple days," Dr. Fenton said.

Rose got up and went to the door. There she stopped and looked back at Dr. Fenton.

"Yes?" Dr. Fenton asked.

"Has he come for me yet?" Rose's voice was like a child's.

"No, he hasn't come for you," Dr. Fenton answered.

Rose nodded and then left.

Five minutes of quiet gave Dr. Fenton time to write several notes down before Dr. Radburn interrupted him.

"Who is she waiting for?" Dr. Radburn asked.

"I don't know," Dr. Fenton answered, "He dropped her off and hasn't been back. She asks about him occasionally, but there isn't much we can tell her."

Dr. Radburn was quiet and didn't interrupt again.

June 18, 2012

Dr. Fenton was staring at the file and ignoring Dr. Radburn as they waited for Rose to arrive for her appointment. Dr. Fenton would have denied Dr. Radburn entry to the therapy sessions, but there was pressure from the board of directors to let Dr. Radburn take them over completely and Dr. Fenton cared too much about the patients to do that to them. So Dr. Radburn was allowed to sit in.

Rose knocked on the door to the room.

"Come in," Dr. Fenton said. Rose entered and sat

down in the chair across from him. She looked at her hands folded in front of her on the table and nothing else. Her hands didn't shake today.

"Good afternoon, Rose," Dr. Fenton said, "How are you today?"

Rose didn't respond or look up.

"How are your roses doing?" Dr. Fenton asked.

Rose glanced at him, but didn't respond. Her eyes were a lot less clear today.

"Is there anything you want to talk about?" Dr. Fenton asked.

Rose didn't respond or look up at him.

"Perhaps another time," Dr. Fenton said. Rose got to her feet and left the room.

"Based on what I have seen of Rose it might be better if she was not given any more medication," Dr. Radburn said, "She seems to be better off the medication than on."

"When Rose is off her medication she gets violent," Dr. Fenton said, "Her medication is merely a sedative to keep her calm. Her violent behaviour puts her in danger as well as others. As the head doctor, I cannot let harm come to the patients if there is any way to avoid it. Also she responds more when on the medication, but not when she is restarting it."

"Very well," Dr. Radburn said.

Dr. Fenton felt like he was dropping the subject for this moment, but would bring it up later.

Dr. Radburn let the subject drop because Dr. Fenton was obviously convinced by his own logic without looking at the present situation. Dr. Radburn had noticed that a lot about Dr. Fenton. There were many patients on medication who would do much better if given a lower dose or taken off the medication entirely. But Dr. Fenton wouldn't listen to suggestions. Mina was the best example of a patient in need of proper therapy and less medication. The therapy sessions were the worst of any patient Dr. Radburn had watched and then there was the complete denial of the effects of the medication. It was almost like Dr. Fenton didn't want his patients to get better.

When Dr. Fenton was forced into retirement and Dr. Radburn was in charge, things would change. Mina would be taken off her medication as well as a few others. Dr. Radburn would focus on wellness for the real patients, rather than just keep them from endangering themselves. Status quo wasn't going to be good enough anymore.

Dr. Radburn's thoughts were interrupted by the next patient arriving for their therapy session.

June 19, 2012

The nurse looked up at the man who had approached the reception desk.

"Can I help you?" The nurse smiled. The man had dirty-blonde hair that fell into his blue eyes. The smile was one-sided with a dimple. He wore blue jeans, white shirt, and a black leather jacket. He had a piece of paper in his hand.

"I'm looking for Rose," The man answered as he rested his hand on the counter part of the desk.

"There is no one on the staff with that name," The nurse answered as she looked at him with confusion.

"She isn't a staff member," The man replied, "She is a patient. She came in about five years ago."

The nurse still looked at him in confusion.

"Five foot six, a hundred and twenty pounds, with long brown hair," The man said.

Recognition slowly came to the nurse's face.

"That Rose," The nurse said.

"There is more than one?" The man asked.

"No," The nurse answered as she reached for the phone, "I'll let Dr. Fenton know that you are here. If you have a seat, I'm sure he'll be down in a moment."

"Thank you," The man said with a nod. He turned and sat down on the couch in the waiting area.

Dr. Fenton wanted to scream and yell at Dr. Radburn as they both stood in his office and Dr. Radburn suggested that Dr. Fenton didn't want to see his patients well. He wanted to point out how blind Dr. Radburn was to the situation of the patients and how much better they were under his care. The only thing that stopped him was the phone ringing.

Dr. Fenton picked it up while glaring at Dr. Radburn.

"Yes," His anger was there because he found that he couldn't do anything about it. The nurse on the other end didn't seem to notice.

"There is a man here to see Rose," The nurse said. Dr. Fenton was about to say something about visiting hours, but then the name clicked in his head.

"I will be right down," Dr. Fenton said before hanging up the phone.

"What was that about?" Dr. Radburn asked. He looked like he was just short of demanding to know.

"A man is here about Rose," Dr. Fenton answered as he made his way around the desk and toward the door.

"But she-" Dr. Radburn started, but Dr. Fenton was out the door and headed down the hallway before he could get any farther. Dr. Radburn closed his mouth and hurried after Dr. Fenton.

They reached the reception desk and the nurse pointed

to the man sitting on the couch flipping through a ten-year-old fashion magazine. Dr. Radburn stayed near the desk as Dr. Fenton went over to the man.

"I'm Dr. Fenton," Dr. Fenton said as he held out his hand. The man looked up at him over the magazine. He closed and put it back on the pile before getting to his feet.

"I'm Finn," The man said, shaking Dr. Fenton's hand, "I'm here to get Rose." The man let go of Dr. Fenton's hand before digging out a piece of paper and offering it to Dr. Fenton. Dr. Fenton took the paper, unfolded it, and looked it over.

"It is going to be a week before you can take her out of here," Dr. Fenton said.

"That is fine," Finn replied, "Can I see her?"

"Yes," Dr. Fenton said, "This way." Dr. Fenton turned and went to the reception desk. He handed the release form to the nurse.

"Get it started," Dr. Fenton told her.

"Of course," The nurse replied as she took the paper. Dr. Fenton headed for the door into the mental hospital itself. Finn followed and Dr. Radburn joined them.

"I am Dr. Radburn," Dr. Radburn said, "I have been helping Dr. Fenton with Rose's care." Finn nodded, but otherwise didn't pay attention to Dr. Radburn, instead focused on where Dr. Fenton was going.

Dr. Fenton went through the hallways of the first floor, avoiding patient areas as he could, to the door that led out to the yard. He reached out and held it open for Finn and Dr. Radburn. Once they were through, Dr. Fenton let the door close.

"Over there," Dr. Fenton pointed toward the rose bushes. Rose was standing there, making sure the roses were fine.

Finn headed toward her. Dr. Fenton stayed where he was and Dr. Radburn was forced to stay there as well. Finn reached Rose and tapped her on the shoulder. Rose turned around. She looked at him with a blank expression. Dr. Fenton started to worry that she wouldn't recognize Finn and then it would be far more difficult to let her leave with him. Then Rose recognized Finn and a smile spread across her face. She hugged Finn and he hugged her back.

Dr. Fenton smiled before turning from the scene. He headed back inside. Dr. Radburn looked confused as he stood there. He was trying to figure out who Finn was and what his connection to Rose was. Dr. Fenton's smile got wider as he thought about how much trouble this was going to cause Dr. Radburn.

He got up and went to the window. It was quiet out there. Maybe the board of directors were right, maybe it was time for him to retire from running the mental hospital. The problem was that Dr. Radburn was not a good person to replace him. Dr. Radburn had no patience and thought he had all the answers even if he had never seen the situation before. Yes, he was right about taking Rose off the medication, but many of the other patients would end up back where they had been when they arrived. That would make everything worse. And teaching Dr. Radburn those things had proven to be impossible.

The phone rang. Dr. Fenton turned from the window and pressed the speakerphone.

"Yes?" Dr. Fenton asked.

"There is a Dr. Gar here to see you," The nurse said.

"I'll be right down," Dr. Fenton said. He pressed the button to turn off the speakerphone. He headed down to the reception desk.

The man Dr. Fenton guessed was Dr. Gar was in his late twenties. He had black hair, brown eyes and the physical dimensions of a student. He was calming down a woman who looked like she was his younger sister. She was agitated because she was in a strange place.

The nurse pointed to the man and nodded when Dr. Fenton looked at her. Dr. Fenton walked toward the chair where the doctor and the woman were. When he stopped close to them, Dr. Gar looked up at him.

"I'm Dr. Fenton. What can I help you with?" Dr. Fenton asked.

"I'm Dr. Gar and this is my sister, Autumn," Dr. Gar said, "Autumn has been through some difficult times recently and I was hoping that she could rest here for a couple days. I was told that this was the best place for people to rest in the whole city. My teachers also talked about the effectiveness of your therapies all the time."

Dr. Fenton looked into those brown eyes and saw truthfulness as well as trust with a little bit of idol worship.

"Intake was a couple hours ago, but let's see what we can do," Dr. Fenton said.

"Thank you," Dr. Gar said.

Dr. Fenton went over to the reception desk. The nurse was already gathering the paperwork.

"Let them know that we have a new patient," Dr. Fenton said, "I believe room 183 is available."

"I'll let them know to get it ready," The nurse said as she handed him the paperwork. Dr. Fenton took the paperwork and turned back to Dr. Gar.

"We need this filled out," Dr. Fenton said, offering the papers to Dr. Gar. Dr. Gar took them and started filling them out.

By the time Dr. Gar was finished the nurse gave Dr.

Fenton the signal that the room was ready. Dr. Gar handed the papers back.

"Thank you," Dr. Fenton said, "I'll take you to her room."

"Come on," Dr. Gar said to Autumn as he held out a hand to help her up. Autumn took his hand and let him help her up, but she wouldn't let go as they followed Dr. Fenton into the mental hospital.

Dr. Fenton led them through the hallways until they reached room 183. The room had been made up for Autumn and there was a nurse waiting. Dr. Fenton sent the nurse away while Dr. Gar got his sister settled into the room. Dr. Fenton let them have their privacy as he waited for them to be done.

Dr. Gar didn't leave his sister alone until he was sure that she was asleep. He stepped out into the hallway and closed the door behind him.

"Thank you for this," Dr. Gar said.

"This is what we do here," Dr. Fenton said.

"I really hope it helps," Dr. Gar said.

"I was wondering if you would be willing to answer some questions," Dr. Fenton said as they started back towards the reception desk.

"I don't mine answering any questions," Dr. Gar said, "I put everything about Autumn I could on the papers."

"I saw that," Dr. Fenton said, "I was wondering when you graduated."

"May of last year," Dr. Gar answered.

"What have you been doing with yourself since then?" Dr. Fenton asked.

"Working with the alcoholics at the hospital," Dr. Gar answered, "It doesn't use much for my skills and education, but it pays the rent and most of the groceries."

"What did you specialize in?" Dr. Fenton asked.

"Clinical mostly," Dr. Gar answered, "A little bit of drug therapy. Why these questions? Are you looking for a new doctor for the hospital?"

They had reached the waiting area. Dr. Fenton moved them away from the reception desk and the nurse's hearing.

"I'm looking for a replacement," Dr. Fenton answered, "I'm thinking of retiring in the next five years and I can't leave these patients without a competent doctor. The board of directors found a doctor they think should replace me, but he has only shown himself to be incompetent. I am supposed to meet with the board of directors this week and tell them that. However, if I don't suggest a doctor who could take over from me they won't listen. You seem competent."

"I don't have the experience to run a mental hospital," Dr. Gar said, "Even if you had done the required background checks." Dr. Fenton could tell Dr. Gar was uncertain even if the idea appealed and excited him.

"I would mentor you into the role," Dr. Fenton said, "I have your contact information, so I can do the background check in the next couple days. Would you be interested in the opportunity?"

"Yes, I would be interested in the opportunity," Dr. Gar said, "If you think I am right for the job.

"I'll do the background check tomorrow and I will call you before I take the recommendation to the board of directors," Dr. Fenton said.

"Okay," Dr. Gar said. Dr. Fenton offered his hand and Dr. Gar shook it.

"Good night," Dr. Fenton said.

"Good night," Dr. Gar replied before heading for the exit. Dr. Fenton watched him leave before turning back to the reception desk and giving the nurse the paperwork.

June 20, 2012

Rose slipped the pill into her hand and swallowed the water as if she was swallowing the pill. She gave both cups to the orderly and shuffled along with the rest of the patients. Most of them shuffled into the dayroom, but Rose didn't follow them. No one paid attention as Rose continued down the hallway.

There was no one in the hallway when she reached the break room and slipped inside. She looked around and saw that it was empty. She started searching for an item she had seen before. Dr. Radburn had a water bottle that she had seen him carry around. Rose found it half full of water in the fridge. She took it out and followed the instructions given to her. She crushed up the pill and put it into the water. Then she put the water bottle back in the fridge. Rose slipped out of the break room and headed outside to her roses.

Dr. Fenton stopped and looked when he noticed someone coming out of the break room. It was Rose. Her eyes were a little clearer for not being on the medication for two days, but she was still lost in her own world the majority of the time. Finn must have told her to do something. She would remember if he asked, but not if anyone else asked.

Dr. Fenton continued on his way. Whatever Rose was doing didn't concern him as much as finishing the background check on Dr. Gar. The meeting with the board of directors was tomorrow and he needed to be ready.

June 21, 2012

"Dr. Radburn," Dr. Fenton called.

Dr. Radburn didn't stop and seemed not to hear his own name.

"Dr. Radburn," Dr. Fenton called louder, but still didn't get any response, "Dr. Radburn!"

Dr. Radburn stopped and looked around. He finally noticed Dr. Fenton and turned to him.

"Yes?" Dr. Radburn asked.

"What is wrong with you?" Dr. Fenton demanded, "You show up two hours late, you just about knock over the medication cart because you didn't notice it, and you haven't done anything that you are supposed to get done."

"I'll get to it," Dr. Radburn said and then turned around and walked away.

Dr. Fenton stayed where he was and watched him go.

"He doesn't drink enough water or fast enough," Rose said from behind Dr. Fenton, "He isn't getting enough at one time for it to have the full effect."

"I'd put it in his coffee, but he would leave it somewhere and never get around to drinking it," Dr. Fenton said.

"He takes pain medicine for his arm," Rose said, "He can't forget pain, so he would take painkillers."

"His arm?" Dr. Fenton asked.

"He winces sometimes if he moves it wrong," Rose said, "Must be a recent injury because he winces multiple time in a day."

"I will see if I can find and exchange his painkillers," Dr. Fenton said, "He is going to be busy until lunch, so I will do it now."

"I'll continue to put mine into his water," Rose said, "The more he has in a day the faster it takes effect."

"As long as it isn't enough for him to overdose," Dr. Fenton said.

"There isn't enough Seraton in the building for him to

overdose," Rose said.

"Good," Dr. Fenton said before heading off to where the medication was kept.

Dr. Fenton straightened his clothes before he opened the door. The board of directors were already seated and waiting.

"Good evening, Dr. Fenton," Director Robertson greeted him as Dr. Fenton took a seat at the table in front of them.

"Good evening," Dr. Fenton responded.

"Where is Dr. Radburn?" Director Robertson asked.

"I have no idea where he is," Dr. Fenton answered, "He disappeared this afternoon and I haven't seen him since. He was also two hours later this morning. He was on time for most of the month. However, he sees all the treatments as slow and useless. He has argued with me over the treatment of several patients who have shown great improvements over the last several months. Many patients avoid him, a few shut down when he is there, and some will attack or act out when he is around."

"You do not think he should replace you," Director Robertson said, "But he was the best candidate that we could find."

"I understand that," Dr. Fenton said, "I also brought a solution."

"Let's hear it," Director Robertson said after glancing around at the other directors to make sure it was okay.

"I have found a young, inexperienced doctor, who had excellent grades and graduated in the last two years," Dr. Fenton said, "I would take five years and mentor him into the position. He would start out with a few jobs and would slowly add more over those years until he does everything I do now. I would show him how to do things, explain certain treatments, and give everyone a chance to get used to him running the mental hospital. At the end of the five years, he would be in control and I would be down to part time counselling work. Then I can retire easily from there."

The directors looked at each other and conferred in whispers for several minutes. Finally Director Robertson looked up at Dr. Fenton.

"Who is this young, inexperienced doctor?" Director Robertson asked.

"Dr. Gar," Dr. Fenton took a file from his stack of papers. He took the file to Director Robertson and set it on the table before going back to his spot.

Director Robertson skimmed it before passing it around. All the directors skimmed it until it got back to Robertson. Then they conferred for several more minutes.

When they were finished, Director Robertson focused on Dr. Fenton.

"We accept this solution," Director Robertson said, "I will be there tomorrow to talk to Dr. Radburn. You can tell Dr. Gar that he starts next Monday."

"Thank you," Dr. Fenton said.

June 22, 2012

Dr. Fenton and Director Robertson found Dr. Radburn at the reception desk as he signed in for the day.

"Director Robertson," Dr. Radburn greeted him with a nod. His hair was sticking up, he had not shaved in two days, and his eyes were having trouble staying in reality.

"Dr. Radburn," Director Robertson acknowledged him. Dr. Fenton checked to make sure that a couple of orderlies were within range to come running to help, just as he had asked. Rose was right about switching the painkillers. It looked like Dr. Radburn had downed half the bottle.

"You were supposed to be here three hours ago," Director Robertson said.

"Oh," Dr. Radburn said. He was confused and probably didn't know what time it was, let alone remember when he was supposed to be there.

"You are fired," Director Robertson said.

A light came on in Dr. Radburn's eyes and he turned toward Director Robertson.

"You can't take this away from me," Dr. Radburn screamed before going for Director Robertson's neck. Dr. Fenton was a second too slow and Dr. Radburn got his hands around Director Robertson's neck.

"Orderlies!" Dr. Fenton yelled as he tried to separate the men. The orderlies rushed in and tried to help, but Dr. Radburn was too strong. The nurse got up and offered Dr. Fenton a needle of tranquilizer. Dr. Fenton took it and injected it into the exposed part of Dr. Radburn's neck.

Dr. Radburn collapsed into the arms of the orderlies, who dragged him away to the ward for dangerous patients. Director Robertson was bent over, trying to get his breath back.

"Come sit down," Dr. Fenton guided him to the chair. Director Robertson sat down and Dr. Fenton got the nurse to call for help.

June 25, 2012

"What did you find out?" Mr. Masters asked the man who had just entered his office.

"Dr. Radburn went nuts and attacked the chairman of the board of directors for the mental hospital," The man answered, "Dr. Radburn has become a patient of the mental hospital for an indefinite period of time. Mina Tate has disappeared, if she was ever there. Both are lost to us."

Mr. Masters was silent. The man left the office to avoid the fury he could feel building. He barely got the door closed before the loud crashes came from inside.

Dr. Fenton was near the reception desk, signing for a package of Seraton when Finn came in, followed by Dr. Gar. They had both arrived at the same time, but obviously didn't know each other. Finn went to Rose, who was sitting on the couch in the waiting room, waiting for him, and Dr. Gar came to the reception desk.

Rose got to her feet as Finn approached. They hugged in greeting. Dr. Gar reached the desk and turned to see what Dr. Fenton was staring at. He saw the kiss. Then Finn and Rose turned to leave. Rose turned back.

"Thank you," Rose said.

"You're welcome," Dr. Fenton replied. Rose smiled before turning back around. She and Finn walked out arm in arm.

"What was that about?" Dr. Gar asked.

"Ten thousand dollars and a deal I wouldn't have turned down for anything," Dr. Fenton answered with a smile, "Come on, I'll give you a tour."

Dr. Gar glanced after Finn and Rose before following Dr. Fenton into the mental hospital.

MOTHERS DON'T GET MEDALS

"I need you to sign this." Her seventeen year old son, Landon, shoves papers under Janice Keller's nose. Janice reaches out to hold them still so she can read them.

"What are they?" She reads the top line before turning to stare at her son, "No."

"Come on, Laura is already at the military academy. How can you object?"

"You have been accepted to Julliard in the fall. I am not letting you throw away the chance of a lifetime to enlist in the army."

"Music is a waste of time, Mom. Going and helping Dad would be a better use of my life."

"Your Dad and I agreed. Your sister is following her interests and getting the education she needs to reach goals we have agreed are right for her. You have musical talent. You have spent years practicing and years studying. You will not give it up because of one old man's teasing."

"This isn't about Jack!"

"I have to go to work. I will not sign this." Janice drops the papers on the counter.

"Dad would sign it." Landon threatens.

"If you can find your father, then ask him." Janice grabs her purse and heads out the door to the base library. She stops and takes a deep breath before heading to the children's department to help young patrons. The morning starts slowly with a storytelling session. It is once the children disperse to find books that she sees the uniformed men waiting for her. She sighs.

"Mrs. Keller, your son, Landon, asked us to speak to you on his behalf." The first man starts.

"Major, my son has been accepted at one of the best schools in the country for musical study. This morning, without any prior warning, he shoves enlistment papers under my nose and demands I sign them. I will not."

"Another few months and your signature will not be required."

"Then he, and you, will just have to wait."

"Are you anti-American, Mrs. Keller?" The other man asks.

"I am fourth generation American army. My great-grandfathers, grandfathers on both sides of the family, father, uncles, aunts, and cousins were or are career soldiers for this country. My husband is off in a combat zone somewhere right at this minute and my daughter is in military academy preparing to join the army. My son is a musician. One old man teases him about not having the courage to die for his country and all the work he has done so he can develop his talent goes right out the window. Not on my signature."

"It is your son's wish."

"Last month I drove my son across three states so he could compete in a classical piano competition. That was his twentieth competition in the last year. He has practiced every day since he was four. Now all of a

39

sudden he wants to toss it all away for boot camp. No, he will regret not taking up a four year scholarship to Julliard for the rest of his life. I will not be responsible for letting that happen!" Janice notices people staring and drops her voice. "I cannot in good conscience sign that. Now, if you do not mind, I have a job to do."

The men frown as Janice walks away.

That night, Janice walks into the small on-base house that she has lived in since her husband took the job in covert operations five years previously. The sound of loud classical music pours from the baby grand piano in the living room. Janice goes to the kitchen to prepare supper.

The music stops and Landon comes to lean in the doorway. "Do you have the entrance fees for the competition next month?"

"Yes, if you still want to compete."

"Of course I want to compete." Landon frowns at her.

"Then I will send in the forms." Janice starts to slice onion.

"Do you have Dad's address?"

"Just send it to his box and the army will forward it." Janice answers.

"Are you still together? I mean it's been over three years since he spent the night here."

Janice tries to think back to the last time her husband had written or called. "He said he had to go deep undercover and I should wait for him to call. Your father will call when he can."

"If I join the army, I can stick around."

"We both know having family nearby is not one of the factors that the army uses when it decides where to deploy people. First there will be boot camp and then postings all over the world. Your father negotiated this place for us when he took this post because he would not be in any one place for long and we could not be with him. He wanted to give us some stability."

Landon frowns. "He could be dead and they wouldn't tell us."

"Yes, they would. We would be served with an eviction notice as soon as they had confirmation. He's still alive and out there." Janice answers. "Send him a letter. Just don't be surprised if it takes a while to get an answer."

"Mom, sign the papers."

"No." Janice shakes her head. "This is one thing you are going to have to do on your own."

"I will get Dad to sign them. He will let me."

Janice just continues to work on cooking supper and Landon slaps the wall. "Sign it!"

"If I sign it then I cannot put you in the competition. They will ship you off to boot camp and a thousand dollars will go to waste. Which do you want Landon, music or army?"

"That's not fair."

"I have spent thousands of dollars on lessons, pianos, and competitions and you want to go stand in front of bullets. What's fair about that?" Janice drops her knife and shifts her fists to either side of her waist.

"You don't understand!"

"Neither do you. And when you do it will be too late for anything but regrets." Janice picks up the knife and continues to chop onions. She moves on to green pepper.

"Julliard is what you want Mom. It is not what I want." Landon flings the words at her.

Janice turns to the ground beef frying in the pan and

adds the vegetables. "If army life is what you want then you are going to have to make it happen without me."

"How am I supposed to do that?"

"That is for you to figure out. Supper will be in an hour."

Landon goes back to the living room and takes his anger and frustration out on the piano.

Janice writes out the check and sends off the entry form the next day. She works and comes home to loud music. She goes out to a support group for army wives, but as the most experienced wife in the group, she answers questions instead of asking them. She goes home feeling hollow.

Landon comes to the table and sits down at his plate. "There's a boot camp starting in three weeks."

"Boot camp has been starting every few months for years and there will be another one in four years if you still think you want to be cannon fodder."

"That's hypocritical. Dad's army. Laura's going to be."

Janice runs the tines of her fork through the rice and chicken mixture in front of her. "Laura did not head straight to boot camp without finishing high school. She chose a field of interest and is studying hard. Her interest is one most used by the military so it makes sense for her to join up when she is done. Your father was drifting and needed the discipline that the army trained into him. Even he would tell you that he went at his career backwards. Neither of them were seventeen. Neither of them are ditching a promising talent to be a private."

Landon frowns and shoves his fork into the food to bring it to his mouth. He finishes his meal in silence before returning to pound out his emotions on the piano. Janice cleans the kitchen. Just as she is finishing, there is a knock at the kitchen door.

Janice looks out the window before going to the door. She opens, steps through, and closes the door at her back. "Go away. You are not welcome here, Jack."

"I saved Mike's life."

"That's no excuse for what you are doing to Landon. You can come back to visit when Mike gets back. Until then you stay away from my home and my son."

"You're babying that boy. In the end he will hate you for it."

"And you are making certain of it. You come around again and I will call the MPs." Janice tells him. "I believe there are still a few outstanding warrants."

The older man goes white. "You bitch!"

"You have two seconds to be gone or I will go to the colonel and point out your record." Janice does not blink until the older man is limping away. She goes back into the house and closes the door softly. Luckily, Landon's music is too loud for him to have heard anything.

Janice rolls over for hours before she gets up and turns on the light in her room. She gets out her special stationary, slightly perfumed and watermarked with light pink roses. She writes her husband of twenty-two years.

Dear Mike,

Jack Fraser has convinced Landon that the only way our son's life counts for something is if he joins the army to help you. I have sent Jack away, but Landon is pressing me to sign his enlistment papers and calling me a hypocrite for not signing. He's even started questioning our marriage in the light of your long absence.

If you could call him, write him, or somehow convince him that going to Julliard isn't unpatriotic. Mothers seem to lose their son's respect after a certain age and I would be grateful for any support you can give me.

Janice.

P.S. I love and miss you.

Janice seals the envelope and addresses it to her husband's post office box. She tucks it into the mail box on her way to work the next morning.

The children are noisy and disruptive during story time, a mother yells at Janice over the choice of book her eight-year old daughter picks out, and her immediate supervisor criticizes her in front of a patron.

Landon is playing one of his own loud creations when she arrives home. Janice goes into the kitchen, but her pounding head makes her too woozy to cook. She sits down with her head on her arms.

That is the way Landon finds her an hour later. "Where's supper?"

Janice manages to raise her head to look at her son before putting it gently back down. "I will get to it when I feel better."

"It's seven o'clock."

"I have a headache. You are going to have to make it for yourself." Janice massages the back of her neck. "There are leftovers from the spaghetti sauce the other night. I am going to bed."

She stands up very carefully and holds on to the walls on her way to her bedroom. She lies down without getting undressed and without turning on the light.

"Mom, are you drunk?" Landon asks.

Janice does not answer with a fervent hope that he will just go away. After a moment of silence, he pulls the door closed and goes.

"Mom, wake up."

Janice opens her eyes just a crack. "What?"

"I made supper. You need to eat something." Landon tells her.

"I don't think I can handle spaghetti sauce." Janice mumbles.

"I made some chicken soup." Landon says. "Well, heated it from a can, really."

"I don't feel like getting up." Janice starts to shake her head, then moans.

"I have a tray, if you could just sit up."

Making the effort costs Janice strength, but she manages to sit against the headboard. Landon sets the tray carefully over her lap. "I added two aspirin and a glass of water."

Bring careful not to knock anything over, Janice starts with the painkillers and then notes the rest of the meal. "Thank you, Landon." She sips the soup slowly, testing her stomach's capacity to handle liquid.

"You could have come told me that you were sick. I could have played softer."

"You need to practice for the concert." Janice takes another sip of soup. "I just had a bad day at work."

Landon frowns. "Is the concert that important if I am just going to join up?"

"I know you are tired of playing other people's works. It takes a lot of discipline and creativity to try to play the same pieces everyone else is playing and somehow make them stand out in the judge's minds. Think of it as getting ready for being a soldier where discipline is paramount."

"Was it really just a bad day at work?"

Janice tries to nod but ends up giving a stiff from the waist movement to stave off the pain in her neck and head. "Thank you for the soup. I need to get ready for bed."

Lifting the tray away, Landon says good night and leaves.

A lingering pain in her head puts Janice on edge as she goes into work the next morning. She takes a deep breath when Johnny Green acts up during story time and listens carefully to all the problems with children's choices for take home books. The last of the pain is almost gone when Janice gets a message to report to the base commander's office.

"Mrs. Keller?" The politely correct young man behind the desk asks.

"I am Mrs. Janice Keller." Janice answers.

"We have had complaints from your neighbours of noise from your house."

"My son plays the piano quite loudly sometimes."

"These are reports of loud voices and fights."

Janice frowns. "When?"

"Last night."

"Last night I had a splitting headache. I spent the evening in a darkened room and never spoke above a whisper. I do not know who filed this complaint, but they were either mistaken in the location or malicious." Janice answers.

"We understand you are at odds with your son."

"I am not in the habit of raising my voice to Landon.

Last night he made chicken soup for my supper after he realized I was ill. There was no yelling on either side."

"You are denying the allegation."

"You can send patrols past my house on a regular basis if you wish. My son plays the piano and sometimes it gets rather loud, especially if he is unhappy as he has been over my refusal to sign his enlistment papers."

"You don't want your son in the army."

"I do not want my son, who is a classical pianist, to dump a scholarship in one of America's most prestigious schools and quit high school short of graduation to join up. My daughter already has her heart set on becoming an officer. One of them in the armed forces should be enough."

The man almost cracks a smile. "I can see your point."

"As far as the neighbours, I do not know what set them off."

The man nods. "Probably the piano."

Janice frowns.

Landon has supper ready when Janice gets home. "How lovely, thank you." She kisses his cheek.

The teen blushes. "I hope you're feeling better."

"I am." Janice sits down. "Landon, have you been having trouble with anyone at school?"

"Not more than usual."

"Usual?"

"There's a guitar player who thinks he's so cool and he wants me to join his band. He does drugs. I avoid him whenever I can. Why?"

"Someone reported yelling and fighting going on at this house last night." Janice frowns.

"Nothing like that happened."

"We both know it." Janice pauses. "I just wondered if it was malicious and directed at you."

"Not that I know." Landon shakes his head.

"Then I do not know what it is about." Janice eats her supper.

"Is it all right if I practice? You still look a little pale. Maybe I should do dishes."

"Go ahead. I am going into my room to read after I do the dishes. The library had a new book by one of my favourite authors on the three day loan rack."

"Thanks. You sure you want to do the dishes?"

"Let me do them as a thank you for a meal I did not have to cook." Janice answers. "You need your practice time."

Landon gets up and goes to the living room while Janice does the dishes and goes to read in her room.

Landon comes to the library one afternoon later that week. "Mom, I have been offered a gig playing in the officer's lounge. The colonel is apparently a classical music fan."

Janice pauses. "How will this affect your practice sessions?"

"I can practice and get paid for it at the same time." Landon almost vibrates with energy.

"It sounds too good to pass up," Janice smiles. "What kind of hours?"

"Five to ten, Wednesday to Sunday. Early enough I can still get up and get to school on time."

"Okay." Janice nods. "You can take it if you keep up with your homework."

"I will." Landon promises. "Thanks, Mom."

Janice comes home to an empty house. She stops

long enough to get herself something to eat and go to the wives' meeting. All the talk ceases when she walks into the room. The women look at their feet rather than making eye contact with her. The questions are more subdued and none are directed at Janice.

Leaving the meeting, Janice sighs and walks home slowly. She gets to the house and lets herself in. She finishes her book from the previous night.

She gets up to check when Landon comes home. "How did the gig go?"

"The gig went fine." Landon answers. "The colonel came in and requested songs. I am going to have to expand my repertoire."

"Landon, has anyone said anything to you today about the complaint thing?"

"Rick, the guy with the band I was telling you about, approached me again. I told him I had a solo gig until the school ends and he seemed shocked. He said he could get me some drugs and I said drugs don't go over well with the colonel. After that he sort of backed away from me."

Janice nods.

"Mom, I have to get to bed. I have about twenty minutes of homework to do tomorrow morning before class."

"Good night then." Janice half-smiles. She goes back to her bedroom and sits down to think.

The next morning Janice goes to work. She manages to get through the day without strange looks or other disturbing events. She comes home to make and eat supper before walking around, feeling empty. She notices some hard water marks on the shower stall. She is still cleaning when Landon comes home.

"Mom, does this place need to be that clean?"

"No, I just did not know what to do with myself." Janice drops the rag back into the bucket of water from where she is scrubbing the kitchen floor. "There are leftovers in the fridge, if you are hungry."

"I bought a burger with my tips. Mom, do you need me home?"

"No, I just need to find a new hobby or a second job."

"The piano is paid for."

"Completely. Although I don't know what I will do with it if you run off to boot camp and I get moved to an apartment."

Landon pales a little. "I need my piano."

"In boot camp you get a cot and a locker. No room for pianos. Or that's how it was when I went through it."

"I never knew you were in the army."

"I was an army brat. I didn't know there was any other way of life until I got posted abroad and was put through cultural sensitivity training. Then I met your father. He joined and I quit to raise you and your sister. I don't think I've lived off an army base in my entire life." Janice sighs. "I will just finish up here and go to bed."

"Mom, you will hang on to the piano?"

"As long as I have room for it."

"Good night, Mom."

"Good night, Landon."

Two weeks go by. Janice works in the library and goes home to her empty house where she is cleaning out closets. One night the phone rings.

"Janice Keller?" A man's voice asks.

"You are speaking to her."

"I understand that you have taught here at the base."

"A number of things. What are you thinking about

precisely?"

"Hand-to-hand combat."

"I am a little out of practice." Janice answers.

"Come over to the gym tomorrow night. I will run you through a circuit and see if you still have what it takes. Believe me, I need the help."

"Who do I ask for?"

"Lieutenant Morris."

"What time?"

"Eighteen hundred hours."

"Okay."

Dressed in comfortable and slightly stretchy pants and a t-shirt, Janice arrives five minutes early the next day.

"I am looking for Lieutenant Morris." Janice tells the man at the reception desk.

"And who shall I say is here?"

"Janice Keller."

"He's expecting you. Go on back." The man points her in the proper direction.

"Class is about to begin." A man yells at her. "Get in line."

Janice moves to the back of a group of young soldiers who are being put through their paces and pushed past their limits. Once they are tired, a man without rank showing arrives.

"Time to find out what you really know."

Five masked men attack the group. Many of the members pull into a circle for safety. Janice chooses a target and puts him down. She yells instructions to the soldiers and the rest of them join the attack.

The man without rank waits for everything to die down. "Men, this is your new instructor, Mrs. Keller."

They salute her. Janice acknowledges them with a

nod.

"Meet here at eighteen hundred hours tomorrow night. Dismissed." Lieutenant Morris addresses the assembly. The soldiers fall out of line and head for the showers.

"Evenings only, no weekends." Janice says.

"Eight weeks and then a live exercise."

"I will go AWOL for a few days. My son has a competition." Janice pauses.

"So long as they are ready in eight weeks."

Landon frowns when Janice explains her second job. "Are you broke? I can spend some of the money I made on getting to the competition."

"No, it is just something to keep me busy in the evening."

"Laura phoned." Landon frowns. "She wanted tuition for a summer training course."

"Did she say if she would phone back?"

"No, she said something about writing Grandpa." Landon rolls his eyes. "She is such a pain sometimes."

"I will phone her." Janice frowns. "It would be nice if you made an effort to get along with your sister."

"After the remarks she makes about me joining up, I don't think so."

Janice reaches for the phone. A young voice from Laura's dorm room says she would pass along the message.

Saturday comes before Janice hears back from her daughter. "You know I can't stay up that late. We have curfews."

"You could phone early." Janice tells her daughter. "Or phone me at the library. The occasional personal call will not get me fired."

"It is too late anyway. I had to get my tuition in before last Wednesday. Now I will have to come home for the summer."

"Your room is clean." Janice tells Laura.

"Mom, have you heard from Daddy?"

"Not lately." Janice pauses. "Why?"

"I sent him a letter weeks ago and haven't got a reply."

Janice thinks about this for a few minutes. "There are lots of reasons why it might take a while to get a reply."

"But he always answers me." She puts special emphasis on the last word. "Can I bring a friend for the summer? I think Daddy would like her."

"I would have to meet this friend first." Janice answers. "You have another eight weeks of school. Another opportunity may arise to do something you like."

"You don't want me home!"

Janice takes a deep breath. "You can come home for the summer. Just don't set your hopes on your father being here."

"In other words, you two have broken up."

"The relationship between your father and me is not up for your speculation. In other words, if you cannot discipline your mouth, I will find you something to do for the summer."

The receiver slams down. Janice pulls the phone away from her ear.

After a long week at the library and the gym, Janice gets home on Friday exhausted. She and Landon arrive at about the same time.

"Mom, you should go to bed." Landon frowns.

"I am, good night, Landon. I intend on sleeping in

tomorrow so make your own breakfast."

"Will do, Mom." Landon nods.

Janice goes off to her room. She manages to change clothes and snuggle under her blanket before her eyes close. She dreams about a phone call from Mike.

The next Monday, when Janice is demonstrating a hold, she notices the needle tracks.

"Soldier, what's your name?" She snaps out the question military style.

"Jerry."

"Jerry what?"

The soldier glances at the person next to him. Janice catches the slightest of shrugs.

"Jerry Vance."

Janice dismisses the class early and heads home. She is waiting when Landon gets home.

"Good night, Mom." Landon leans against the wall nearest his bedroom.

"I have some questions for you."

Landon frowns but nods. "Go ahead."

"Do you know a Jerry Vance?"

"Yeah, he's in my English class. What's this about?"

"Who does he hang out with?"

"Rick and his band friends."

"Have these guys changed their hair style in the past few weeks?"

"Yeah, one of them complained rather loudly about his father demanding a brush cut." Landon runs his hand threw his longish hair. "I'm glad you don't do that to me. Even the colonel hasn't said anything."

Janice nods. "How is the gig going?"

"Good, the colonel told me how the lounge got its piano. He bought it for his children and none of them played it even though they had lessons. I can't imagine having a piano and not playing it."

Janice smiles, "No, I don't think you could. Good night, Landon."

"Good night, Mom."

An early morning visit delays Janice getting to work. She goes right into story time. Books are selected before she goes to the desk, but no one notes her absence. She is getting off for the day when two MPs accost her at the front desk.

"Mrs. Keller."

"Yes."

"We would like to speak to you about what was reported to us." The same man speaks both times.

Janice grabs a key to a small meeting room. "Do you want a formal statement or just information?"

"A formal statement would be preferred."

"Come with me." Janice leads the way to the private room.

"We want you to go to the gym as usual and we will be right behind you." The talking MP tells her.

Janice nods. "I have been changing here, before I leave the library. If you will give me a few minutes in the ladies room."

She changes quickly and, at their wave, leads the way to the gym. The guy at the front desk waves her back as usual. Janice takes a deep breath and steps into the room. Everyone is there except Lieutenant Morris.

"Where's the lieutenant?"

"He said he would be a little late." One of the soldiers says.

"Then we will start with a twenty minute run with

intervals very second circuit." Janice raises her voice. "Go." She runs beside the last man and she pushes him. That pushes the ones in front of him. The intervals are even faster.

Lieutenant Morris enters after eighteen minutes and frowns at the exhausted men. "What?"

"All present and accounted for." Janice calls out.

A dozen MPs enter and take everyone into custody. The young soldiers are no trouble as they have no breath left to fight.

"Mrs. Keller, we owe you our thanks," Colonel Riley says, "Both for your assistance in breaking the drug ring and in giving us a very good pianist for the lounge."

"Until you know what they were planning, I don't think I broke anything, and Landon has done all the work. I just provided the encouragement."

"Encouragement is sometimes hard to find." Colonel Riley pauses. "I understand you bought him a baby grand."

"Only once I knew he was serious about playing every day." Janice answers. "He has really appreciated having an interested audience."

"Still, I wish to thank you. We are going to have to put those young men through rehab."

Janice just nods.

Rather than going back to empty evenings, Janice spends a Saturday off base and returns with enough sewing projects to last her into retirement. She digs out her old sewing machine and sets up her bedroom as a place to sew, leaving only enough room to sleep and dress.

She also returns to the wives' meetings. The other

women look uncomfortable.

"What's eating you?" Janice demands of another woman.

"You wouldn't sign Landon's enlistment papers. You protect your baby while our husbands suffer."

"My son would never make it as a soldier."

"And you are the expert how?" The women move to form a solid wall against her.

"I am fourth generation professional army. I spent five years in the military, starting the day after I graduated high school. I know army and my son is not cut out for army life. It would be a waste of his talent. Just because a child gets an idea in his head does not mean it is a good one."

"So he gets off with a free pass." A woman with an ID tag saying she is Mrs. Bower curls her lip.

"Only if you call sitting at a piano for at least five hours a day, every day, since he was four, a free pass." Janice pauses.

The woman's eyes widen and her mouth forms an O. Then a hard look comes into her eyes. "You still got no right choosing for him."

"I know my son and the army is not the right place for him." Janice answers.

The jaws of half a dozen women tighten. Janice turns around and walks out of the meeting.

Besides her job, Janice goes nowhere for the next two weeks. Landon knocks on her bedroom door.

"Come in." Janice calls as she pins quilting pieces into place.

"Mom, are you coming to my competition?" Landon leans against the wall.

"Yes, it's the week after next on Friday night. I have

not forgotten. I just seem to get into trouble if I leave the house."

Landon pauses. "I heard rumors about what happened with the other wives. Why is it so important to them for me to go to boot camp?"

"Misplaced loyalty." Janice frowns.

"The colonel said he wants to come to the competition, so he was asking if I wanted a ride with him."

"How do you feel?"

"I guess I'm superstitious. I want it like it always has been." Landon bites his lip.

"We will make it like it always has been." Janice tells him.

"Thanks Mom." Landon comes and gives her a quick hug. "Good night."

"Good night."

At the library the next day, Janice books herself off for three days at the end of the following week before going to story time. Her supervisor comes over as soon as the majority of the children leave.

"Three days? Isn't that overkill?"

"It's the last competition before Landon turns eighteen. It is two days drive and one day for practice before he competes. Exactly the same as we have done for every other competition."

"If he's going to Benning-"

"I have three weeks of holiday coming. I am taking three days. I will go over your head if it is necessary to get approval."

The supervisor frowns. "You don't deal with authority very well."

"I don't deal with meddling very well. Real authority,

I respect." Janice answers.

The supervisor snaps his mouth shut. "If you must take off three days."

"I must."

Janice is at home when Laura phones.

"Mom, you were right something else did come up."

"What?"

"A cadet camp."

"And what are the fees?"

"No fees, I am teaching. They wanted someone with academy training to teach orientation." Laura answers. "I scored highest in their testing."

"Congratulations." Janice puts a smile into her voice.

"I've got everything I am going to need here. I might have a week at the end of summer to come home."

"Time to shop for the next year at the academy."

"Mom, is Landon really going to enlist?"

"I hope not, but after he turns eighteen there is nothing I can do to stop him." Janice answers.

"I can just see him telling some master drill sergeant 'I will get there after I practice piano'." Laura tries to mimic her brother's voice.

"Jack Fraser was here trying to convince Landon that being a musician meant he wasn't a real man. I hope I got rid of his influence."

"Jack Fraser? Wasn't he blacklisted from bases?" Laura replies.

"Around the world."

"I have to go, curfew."

"Have a good time with the cadets." Janice tells her.

"First exams, then cadets." Laura allows the change of subject. "I spoke to Grandpa. He said not to give you a bad time."

"Thank your grandfather for that." Janice answers. "Landon and I will be away for a few days. He has his last competition for the school year."

"Wish him luck." Laura says before she hangs up.

Janice locks the house and goes to join Landon in the car. They drive for twelve hours and find a hotel. The next day is the same, only they check into the same hotel as the rest of the contestants. Landon goes off to register his presence and find his place on the practice schedule. Janice gets them unpacked. She goes to listen to all his practices. There are no deviations allowed from the other competitions.

No one says anything to Janice the whole time. It is only after the competition when the colonel comes up to her. "Excellent playing."

"I think his time in the lounge playing for other people has helped him." Janice nods.

Landon finds them standing in the aisle of the auditorium. "Mom, they want me to stay and be part of the next group. Can we stay? It will take until Tuesday."

"I have to work on Monday."

"I have some pull. I think I can get you another few days." Colonel Riley offers.

"Then yes, we can stay."

Landon's grin gets even larger. "I need to practice a new piece. I've got to get my new practice schedule." He heads off.

"I have never seen someone so keen on playing the piano." Colonel Riley shakes his head.

"When his Dad teased him at eight about wanting a car at sixteen, Landon asked for a grand piano instead." Janice answers. "This is why I could not sign his enlistment papers."

"I heartily agree. That boy is not meant for the army."

The second competition is tough; the competitors more focused and able to wring emotions out of the keys with full body workouts as a side effect. Landon turns to a piece that he plays when he is upset. Janice listens, but can find no fault with the performance. She sits perfectly still while the winners are announced for the bronze medal, the silver medal, and the gold metal. Landon's name is not announced.

"Ladies and gentleman, we have a very special award tonight for a young man whose accumulated points for the last year have won him not only a scholarship to Julliard but a contract to play with philharmonic orchestras all over the country. Although just seventeen and not yet graduated from high school, he has shown discipline and a love for piano that is head and shoulders above his peers. Help me in congratulating Landon Keller."

The whole audience jumps to its feet while Janice is wondering if she has heard correctly.

Landon goes to the stage.

Placing her hand across her mouth, Janice finally rises to her feet.

"We have a tutor ready to help Landon through his last six weeks of school. Depending on the date, we will fly him back to attend his graduation with his classmates. Now until he goes to Julliard, he is booked for a concert a week. It is a special tour with other young musicians who are outstanding for their age."

Janice turns to her son. "You have worked your whole life for this if it is still what you want."

Landon cringes. "You can't say no now."

"I am not saying no. I am asking you to state plainly that this is what you want."

"I want it," Landon answers. "No ifs, buts or maybes."

"Then I will sign the papers." Janice tells him. Landon hugs her.

Janice and Landon drive home, but he stays only to pack his bags and catch a Greyhound. Janice is in the library when Mrs. Bower enters.

"I hear Landon left for boot camp."

Janice finishes helping the young patron while the woman waits for an answer.

"Boot camp doesn't start for another week." Mrs. Bower pushes.

"Has your son signed up? Is that how you know?" Janice asks.

The woman glares at Janice. "That's none of your business."

"And Landon is none of yours. If you will excuse me, I need to help a patron." Janice walks over to a child eyeing the book shelf with uncertainty.

Mrs. Bower follows. Janice bends down to speak with the girl. Janice's supervisor comes over. "Is there a problem?"

"I asked Mrs. Keller a question, and I am waiting for an answer."

"Unless it is about library services for children, Mrs. Keller is working. I suggest you set an appointment to speak to her outside her work hours."

Mrs. Bower glares at him and leaves.

Janice glances up. "Thank you."

The supervisor blinks in surprise, but nods and goes

back to the children's desk.

Moving her sewing projects to the living room and the dining room, Janice makes quilts over the next few weeks. She is working on a backing when the doorbell rings.

Janice glances out the window at a crowd scene. She notes Mrs. Riley, the colonel's wife, and opens the door. "Happy Birthday!" The ladies yell.

"Give me a moment to clear the living room." Janice heads back into the house to carefully stack the pieces of cloth in some sort of order. She puts them on the piano to leave space on the couches and dining room table. The women file into the kitchen and start taking out glasses and small plates. They move into the dining room and filter into the living room.

"A grand piano." One of the mothers of younger children touches the finish with awe.

"A baby grand." Janice answers.

"Do you give lessons?" Another woman asks.

"I don't play. I bought it for my son." Janice shakes her head. "If you can find someone who does and wants to teach, they can use it for an hour or so in the afternoon."

"That's so generous." The mother of younger children says.

"Landon's no longer here to play it, but I promised him I would hang on to it as long as I had space." Janice answers. "I don't think it does it any good just to sit there."

Another woman frowns. "You live here by yourself? I thought there were regulations."

"Technically, there are four of us. My husband is deployed overseas, my daughter is at military academy, and my son is not yet of age and may return at any time." Janice shrugs. "They are just not here right now."

Mrs. Riley steps into the conversation. "This is why we are here to help you celebrate a birthday when we thought you might be alone. We brought birthday cake and something to drown your sorrows."

"Thank you." Janice eats cake, but avoids eating anything else.

"So where is your husband?" Another woman from the wife's group asks.

"Deployed overseas." Janice answers.

"But where overseas?" Her questioner frowns.

"I am not at liberty to discuss my husband's whereabouts."

"Is that what Landon is doing as well?" Mrs. Bower, who arrived late, dives into the conversation.

"My husband tells me that Landon won both a prestigious scholarship and a contract to play classical music all over the country. He is a boy that makes this base proud. Too bad some of our other children are not as disciplined." The colonel's wife faces down Mrs. Bower.

"Maybe some of us can't afford baby grand pianos." Mrs. Bower curls her lips. "It makes me wonder where they got the money."

"I work at the library. You know, where you accosted me the other day." Janice answers.

Mrs. Riley interrupts. "It's time to wind this party down. In case her husband or children phone."

The ladies clean up mostly by taking their dishes with them when they go. Janice is relieved to close the door behind them. She spreads out her sewing and goes back to work. The phone rings.

"Hello."

"Janice, it's your father." The gruff voice is recognizable.

"Hi, Dad."

"I thought someone should remember your birthday. Mike's off in the Middle East."

"I am not supposed to know that, Dad."

"Military secrecy. Hardly worth the bother now the press puts pictures on the internet as everything is happening. What's this I see about a Landon Keller playing solos with the Arizona philharmonic?"

"He won a contract. He's playing all over the country, and then going to music school."

"Never could make a man of him."

Janice takes a deep breath and counts to ten.

"Do you suppose they would sell a ticket to a retired military man?"

"If you have the cash, yes."

"Don't have anything else to spend my pension on now your mother has passed on."

Janice bites the inside of her mouth to keep from speaking.

"Just phoned to wish you a happy birthday." The phone goes dead. Janice hangs it up and goes to change for bed.

Janice reaches for a storybook the next morning.

"Mommy says you have a piano at your house." A little girl eyes Janice as if she is deciding on her trustworthiness.

"I do." Janice nods.

"Is it a nice piano?" The girl tilts her head to one side.

"My son likes it." Janice answers.

"Can I come see it?"

"If your mother comes with you, you can come."

The little girl gives Janice a timid smile and races off to her mother.

A knock on the door just as Janice closes the cupboard door after putting the clean dishes away brings Janice up right. She goes to look out the window, but it is the little girl and the woman who had admired her piano at the birthday celebration.

Janice opens the door and invites them into the house.

"Sorry about coming at the supper hour, but Cheryl has an early bedtime."

"I am finished. Come into the living room." Janice leads the way.

Cheryl reaches out her hand, but stops short of touching the instrument. Janice opens the key cover. "Sit down on the bench."

"She might damage it."

"After Landon, I doubt she is strong enough to knock it out of tune." Janice shrugs.

Cheryl climbs up on the bench and very softly plinks the keys. The last note is out of place.

"Sorry."

"That is what practice is for." Janice tells Cheryl. "Even good players hit a wrong note sometimes."

Cheryl gives her a half smile and goes back to plinking the keys. When she is finished, she slides off the bench. "Thank you. It's a very nice piano."

"You are welcome." Janice tells the child.

"Could I come back again?" Cheryl glances at her mother and then adds, "Please."

"You could. Your mother and I would have to talk about when." Janice nods.

"It's time to go home for now. Bedtime." Cheryl's mother says.

Janice sees them to the door.

"May we speak again about lessons?" Cheryl's mother asks.

"The only obstacle is finding someone to teach her." Janice answers.

"Thank you."

Janice is forced by necessity to visit the commissary to buy groceries Saturday morning. She is half-way down the baking aisle when Mrs. Bower comes towards her. Janice ignores the woman as she picks up flour and baking powder.

"Mrs. Keller!"

"I'm busy." Janice tells her and pushes her cart down the aisle. The woman dogs her footsteps.

"You are breaking regulations."

Janice picks up a jar of jam and pushes her cart to the next aisle. She does not answer the woman's repeated attempts to speak to her and to accuse her of various misdeeds. Janice is about at the limit of her patience when she gets to the till. Janice starts unloading her cart. Mrs. Bower tries to get between Janice and the counter.

"You are going to listen to me."

Janice takes a final deep breath.

"Captain Bower, what are you doing?" The sergeant in charge of the commissary comes over. "And why are you out of uniform?"

"Stay of this, sergeant. It's not your business." Mrs. Bower suddenly takes the offensive.

"You are harassing one of my paying customers. This is my business." The man answers. "Now get out of the way."

"I will report this."

"No, I will report this." The sergeant reaches for a telephone attached to the check out. "This is Tony from the commissionaire. I have an out of control officer who is harassing my customer. Send an MP."

Captain Bower glowers at the sergeant, but he pulls her aside. "Help this customer with her order." He tells the clerk. "She has been delayed enough for one day."

The colonel's office phones and Janice goes over there.

"Mrs. Keller." The man who had spoken to Janice about the noise complaint approaches her.

"Yes."

"The colonel would like your statement about what happened this morning with Captain Bower." He escorts her to a desk.

"Do you want a statement or do you want to ask questions?"

"We can start with a statement and then I might have a few questions."

Janice nods. "Mrs. Bower, or at least that is who she introduced herself as, has been coming to the spouse of soldier's meetings for a number of weeks. I stopped going after I refused to sign my son's enlistment papers because the wives insisted I was wrong to do so. Mrs. Bower showed up at the base library where I work to question me about the whereabouts of my son. My supervisor sent her away. This morning, when I went grocery shopping, she chased me down most of the aisles, questioning everything from my living accommodations to my children. Sergeant Trainor stopped her when she stood between me and the counter when I was attempting to check out. I did not know until then that she was military personnel."

The man frowns. "Mrs. Keller, I have not met your husband. What does he do?"

"My husband is not attached to this base. He's overseas."

The man pauses. "Excuse me a moment." He gets up and leaves the room then returns with a file. He opens it and reads through the information. He whistles and then glances back at Janice.

"You are free to go."

The ringing of the telephone interrupts Janice's sewing.

"Keller residence." Janice glances at the clock which tells her it is late.

"Sweetheart."

"Mike."

"I got your note. Is Landon there?"

"No, but he's not at boot camp either. He has a contract to play piano until he goes off to Julliard."

"What happened?"

"He was chosen to play with a group of other young promising musicians for a tour of philharmonic orchestras. Suddenly he discovered his love of music again."

"What about Laura?"

"She has a job teaching cadets for the summer."

"That leaves you all alone."

"I'm spending my time sewing quilts I always promised myself I would make and working at the library."

"Sounds lonely."

Janice pauses. "I'm an army brat, remember, and an only child. I am used to it."

"It's time I came home."

"My fault for getting you mixed up in the military." Janice blinks back tears. "Sorry for alarming you over Landon."

"It's not you who should be apologizing. I haven't been a very attentive father."

"He will be fine. His music grounds him."

"His mother's good sense grounds him."

"I'm not sure that's it. Laura still takes all her moods out on me. There's no grounding there."

"Laura is a brat and always has been." Mike answers. "Don't take anything she has to say to heart. Anything else happening?"

"Nothing for you to worry about." Janice answers. "Just look after yourself."

"Now I am worried."

Janice tries to laugh but it comes out broken. "I'm not very popular at the moment. Landon got a little loud about my not signing his enlistment papers and some of the wives thought I was wrong not to sign them."

"Damn busybodies."

"It doesn't matter. It gives me more time to sew."

"Janice, you need a support group."

"There's no support there. I still have work to keep me busy. Don't worry, I will be here when you get back."

"I can phone Hardy and get you a move."

"But then I would have no place for Landon's piano. I promised him I would keep it as long as possible. Laura is close enough to come home if she needs me. Some place new is not always better. I moved enough to know that."

"What happened with Jack Fraser?"

"I sent him away. Told him to stay away from Landon." Janice answers.

"Jack has some powerful friends."

"I will deal with it. You have enough to think about without Jack. I want you back alive and that means no distractions." Janice tells him.

"Janice, you are out of the line of command."

"Which means I do not have to obey orders. I do not have to submit to their nonsense and I can find creative solutions."

"Damn, I have to go. Please, find a friend. Someone you can talk to." The line cuts out.

The library is quiet the next afternoon when Cheryl's mom enters. "Mrs. Keller, I found a piano teacher. He gives lessons off base, but he says he will come two days a week if I can get access to a piano."

"What's his name?"

"Eric Miner."

"I have seen him at student recitals. Tell him that you have access to the piano from after school to five o'clock. I will have to find you a house key."

"I know you are getting tired of hearing it, but thank you. It's just she's such a daddy's little girl and he's been gone for weeks. Learning music seems to be the only thing that interests her."

"Then I am glad I can provide the piano." Janice tells her. "Come by one night after five and I will find you a key."

Janice's supervisor looks over and frowns.

"I will go so you don't get in trouble." Cheryl's mother says.

Janice moves her quilting into the dining room so the living room is free. She finds a key and leaves it where she can get it easily. She checks in the fridge for leftovers before deciding that she really should make supper. She eats two of the chocolate chip cookies she had bought for Landon instead and then just feels sick.

The doorbell rings. Janice goes to answer it. It is Cheryl and her mother. Janice opens the door. "Come in."

"I don't want to be a bother." Cheryl's mother looks upset.

"Come in. I could use the company. I'm not used to living alone." Janice tells her. "What's wrong?"

"The people upstairs are fighting again." Cheryl tells her. "Then Mom's tummy starts to hurt and it's not good for the baby."

"Hush, Cheryl."

Janice points Cheryl towards the living room and then takes her mother by the arm to follow. "Come in and rest."

"Can I play the piano again?"

"Yes, you may." Once Cheryl's mother is sitting on the couch, Janice comes over to open the lid over the keys and help Cheryl onto the stool. The girl starts plinking and Janice goes back to sit beside her guest.

"You're pregnant?"

"About three and a half months."

"You are living in the apartments?"

"You have to understand, Derek just barely finished boot camp before he took this mission. I got so sick before Cheryl was born. He said we needed the money from his deployment, just in case."

"The people upstairs?"

"A single mom and her teenaged sons, who fight about everything when they are not throwing parties. I can't afford anything better. We lost everything when Derek lost his job last year. Derek is doing his best."

"How were you going to pay for music lessons?"

"I will find work. I used to run a daycare in our house until the bank took it back. Someone must need a babysitter."

"The base has its own daycare." Janice shakes her head. "What other skills do you have?"

"Before I got married. I worked in a call centre answering telephones."

Janice frowns. "Is it morning sickness or something worse?"

"Right now, it's like morning sickness, only it's morning, noon and night. It's worse than it was with Cheryl. I had to quit work with her."

"Do you know of anything that would settle your stomach?"

"No, I feel like such a wimp."

"Have you made supper for Cheryl?"

"I couldn't. The smell of cooking food makes me sick. I am a horrible mother. And she will only eat two bites anyway."

"I haven't really eaten yet. I will make something simple and you can join me." Janice answers. She goes into the kitchen and makes vegetable soup which she serves to her guests with crackers.

Cheryl eats her soup quickly, then asks if she can play the piano again. Janice smiles and gives the child permission. Cheryl's mother pushes her uneaten soup away.

"Nibble on a cracker. That's reputed to help with morning sickness." Janice tells the young woman. "First, my name is Janice. And yours is?"

"Sharma Burnett." The young woman answers.

"Sharma, have you gone to the doctor?" Janice asks.

Sharma nods. "Derek insisted on it when the home

pregnancy test came out positive. He said that we couldn't take any chances after I was so sick with Cheryl."

"Have you gone back to all the checkups?"

"Derek phones and asks about what the doctor said so I can't not go." Sharma admits. "He's a great dad, even if we hadn't planned on me getting pregnant right now."

Janice nods. "And what does the doctor say about this sickness?"

"He says it's stress and I need to find new living conditions, but the money only stretches so far with rent and groceries and now Cheryl wanting piano lessons." Sharma answers.

"Perhaps we can do each other a huge favour." Janice answers. "My husband is deployed overseas, my daughter is off teaching cadets for the summer, and my son has a multicity tour with philharmonic orchestras. The piano belongs to my son and if I have to move I can't keep it, but I may have to move if I am here alone. So if you and Cheryl want to use my son and daughter's bedrooms then I can honestly say that I am not here alone. That way I can keep the piano and get you away from the stress and we can negotiate the rent to something where you can still afford music lessons without requiring you to get a job that your doctor would advise against."

Sharma frowns. "I don't want charity. Derek would get upset. He's a proud man."

"It's not charity. Do you know what a baby grand piano is worth? I spent years working to pay that piano off and storage for it would be more than rent on your apartment. Landon begged me to hang onto his piano before he left. I can only do that if I have someone else living here." Janice answers. "You think about the offer and talk to Derek and your doctor about it. For now Cheryl needs an audience. We will go listen to her play."

They listen for an hour to Cheryl before Sharma insists that the little girl needs to get home to bed. Janice gives Sharma a key to the house and then spends the rest of her evening quilting before going to bed after her company leaves.

It is the next afternoon when someone from the base office comes to the library to find Janice.

"Mrs. Kellar, we understand you offered to rent Sharma and Cheryl Burnett empty bedrooms in your house." The uniformed man starts.

"Yes, for now my family is away and I am not used to living alone." Janice pauses. "Is there some trouble in doing so?"

"No, no trouble. Dr. Reid just wanted to make certain that the offer was real. Mrs. Burnett's medical condition is serious and if this is a legitimate offer then he wants her to take it. He is worried that she might lose the child if she continues to live in the conditions she is now."

"Yes, the offer is legitimate." Janice answers. "She can move in today unless it takes longer to move her belongings."

"What time will you get home so she can get in?"

"I gave Sharma a key so her daughter could play the piano when she wanted. I just have to clear the bedrooms of my children's belongings. I get off at five." Janice answers.

"We will arrange to have Mrs. Burnett's things moved to the house at five." He says and leaves.

Janice goes home after work to find three soldiers unloading household goods into her house. Cheryl comes running the moment she sees her. "Are we really going to live at your house?"

"Yes, you are. Do you want to see your new bedroom?" Janice asks.

The child nods. Janice takes her to Landon's room. One of the soldiers follows her. There is a wall that displays Landon's medals and trophies.

"What are those?" The little girl asks.

"Those are the awards my son won in piano competitions." Janice says.

"Can they stay there? I promise not to touch them." Cheryl asks.

The fact that the prized possessions are behind glass makes this promise far more likely to be kept.

"If you don't mind them there then it is easier to leave them there." Janice answers. "The bed and dresser can go downstairs." Janice tells the man. She takes him and the girl out to show him the door to the basement.

"We should go talk to your mother." Janice tells the child.

"She's lying down on the couch. The doctor insists she get lots of rest." Cheryl answers and skips toward the living room.

Janice follows her to find Sharma sitting not laying on the couch. "Once I mentioned your offer to the doctor, he wouldn't let me say no."

"Did you talk to Derek?" Janice asks.

"I didn't get a chance." Sharma sighs. "What if he says no?"

"How long is he to be gone?" Janice asks.

"Six months, but he only left two weeks ago." Sharma answers.

"Then you have five months to rest and two weeks to find another apartment if he wants one when he arrives back." Janice answers. "I have to go see what my daughter left in the bedroom."

76

ONCE A THIEF

Wind Valley, July-10

Of the four seated around the table in the large, elegantly decorated dining room, only the three men are actually eating. The woman is sipping her rapidly cooling tea without touching the contents of her plate. The only sounds are of cutlery on dishes. Or at least until one of the men speaks.

"Did she take anything?"

A second man glances up at the speaker, "Her blade."

"She'll be okay then." The first man nods to himself.

"You really think so?" The woman frowns, clearly concerned.

"She needs some time and space..." The second man takes a deep breath, "Honestly, so do I."

"Meaning?" The woman continues to frown.

"Will and I leave for Belstrand tomorrow. We'll be back when we're ready."

"You'll look for her then?" The first man guesses.

"Long as I'm still able to track her down."

"And if you can't for some reason?" The woman demands.

The first man shakes his head, "She won't be hard to find when she's needed."

* * *

Settlement City, November-61

The wind blows scraps of garbage along the alley. Several people huddle down in ragged blankets and other scrap cloth. All of them shiver except for one petite form.

The figure is female, seemingly in her teens, with long, matted, blonde hair and eyes like the cold wind. She is wearing a loose, ragged t-shirt and ancient dark jeans. Her arms, feet, and head are bare. She crouches down against a brick wall, not seeming to see anything around her.

A ragged small child comes running into the alley and launches herself at one of the shivering heaps of blankets. Fabric wrapped arms emerge to pull the child inside the blankets. Moments later, giggling can be heard. Most of the cold faces around them break into smiles. The petite female rises to her feet and walks away.

The silent petite figure pauses at the alley entrance. Pale, cold eyes take in the scene in front of her.

Two ragged women are doing their best to shelter a small girl from a heavy set man wielding a large handgun. Both women are pleading and crying. The child is cowering and whimpering.

Before the petite female can react, the gun goes off twice and the women fall. The child bolts, narrowly evading the man's reach, right into the petite female. The small girl stumbles as the man lunges towards them. Suddenly, something silvery flickers through the air and he falls.

The petite female approaches the prone form and kicks it over. Reaching down, she retrieves a knife and wipes the blade clean on his clothes. The knife vanishes as the petite female turns to leave the alley.

The small girl is shaking as she slowly gets up. She eyes the petite female warily. Then her eyes go to the fallen women. Before she can start towards them, the petite female catches her. The small girl kicks and struggles, but cannot break free. The petite female holds on until the small girl falls limp.

The garbage littered alley looks nearly identical to any other alley in the neighbourhood except for a single symbol roughly scratched into the wall beside the far door. As they approach, the petite female checks on the small girl in her arms. The child is still unconscious. At the end, the petite female shifts the child enough to allow her to raise one hand to knock. A cold wind whips along the alley, redistributing the garbage and causing the unconscious child to shiver.

Finally, the door opens just enough to reveal a poorly dressed, irritated looking woman, who eyes those outside warily, "Wha' d'you want?"

The petite woman shifts the child to one arm so she can pull up the left sleeve of her t-shirt to reveal a tattoo. The woman in the doorway studies it with a rising eyebrow.

"That doesn't entitle either of you to anythin'. Not here," She scowls, "Not when we can't even feed our own."

The petite female raises a sceptical eyebrow, allowing her sleeve to drop and shifting her hold on the child again.

"What?" The other woman's scowl deepens, "Times 're hard an' the Church spares no quarter for those beneath their notice."

Cold eyes study her critically, but the woman's expression only grows darker. Finally, the petite female shakes her head and turns away. As she walks the length of the alley, she can hear the door slam.

The small girl in her arms stirs as they leave the alley, but does not wake. The petite female keeps walking, her eyes glancing over the buildings around them. Eventually, one heavily boarded up old shop catches her eye. She glances over what can be seen of the front before circling around to see what there is for a back door. What she finds is a basement entrance with a heavy duty padlock on the door. The concrete steps going down to the door are crumbling and the landing at the bottom is layered with indistinguishable debris, some of which is sharp even to the petite female's hardened feet.

Setting the still sleeping child on a relatively clear step, the petite female fishes a piece of old wire from the mess and bends it into the shape she wants. She uses the makeshift tool to pick the padlock, which she sets aside. When she tries the door, it sticks in the frame, requiring a hard yank to open. Once it is open, she steps into the doorway to survey what can be seen of the dark space by the light from outside.

Old boxes and crates are stacked haphazardly and there is a strong smell of old alcohol mixed with dust. There are no visible windows and the whole space appears to be one open area, which is only a little warmer than outside.

The petite female scoops up the child and carries her inside. Setting the small girl by the wall, just inside the door, the petite female pulls the door tightly closed and locks it from inside using the deadbolt. Once her eyes adjust to the near complete blackness, she turns her attention to checking the contents of the crates and boxes, most of which turn out to be empty. The full ones are stacked into a wall to prevent access to the inside stairs. The rest are moved against one end wall, leaving most of the floor open. Once that is done, the petite female pauses in the middle of the floor to survey the dark space.

A whimpering comes from beside the door and rapidly grows into a full blown cry. The petite female goes over to the small girl, crouching down beside her and reaching out to rest a hand on the matted hair.

"So dark." The girl clings to the arm, tears pouring down her face.

The petite female purses her lips momentarily before standing and helping the child to her feet. She takes one small hand in hers before unbolting and opening the door. Outside, she replaces the padlock, ensuring it is securely in place.

"What is this place?" The girl looks up uncertainly.

The petite female does not respond. Nor does she loosen her grip on the child's hand as they mount the steps.

On the street, they walk in a seemingly random direction and are soon mingling, barely noticed, with the other pedestrians in a busier part of town. Eventually, their route takes them into an alley where both lean against a wall. The petite female empties her jeans pockets, coming up with three fat wallets. She quickly rifles through them, pocketing the cash and tossing away everything else. The small girl also empties her pockets, shrinking a little under cold eyes as she sifts through wrapped hard candies, pens and other small items of little value. The petite female slowly shakes her head as the child tucks her treasures back away.

The two link hands again before leaving the alley and walking to a junk shop near the abandoned building they had visited earlier. When they enter, the clerk eyes them warily. The petite female guides the small girl over to a chair near the till and sits her in it with a silent warning to not move. The child grips the edge of the chair, shivering under the wary eyes of the clerk, as she watches the petite female move around the shop.

She picks through a mountain of questionable looking bedding before finally selecting two sleeping bags and several of the best blankets. Those are brought over to the counter and piled beside the till. Next, she rifles through rack after rack of clothing, slowly gathering an armful of garments which are eventually piled with the bedding. Then she picks up a battery operated lantern and any useful batteries. Lastly, she moves to a bin of miscellaneous kitchen items and selects a few things. Once she brings those over to the till, she produces the wad of bills from her pocket. The clerk rings up the sale, names a total, and accepts the approprate bills. The whole pile of items is packed into a box, which the petite female takes. She indicates for the child to accompany her in leaving the shop.

The two of them walk back to the abandoned building where the petite female picks the padlock and opens the door. Inside, they unpack the box. Once the lantern is working, the sleeping bags and blankets are turned into two fairly cosy beds in one corner. The clothes are sorted out into what will fit the child and what will fit the petite female. Then each picks an outfit to change into.

The small girl pulls on a long sleeved tunic over

fleece pants. There are also boots and a lined felt coat with a hood. The petite female slips into a fitted black leather vest which zips up the front. That is paired with black jeans and slip on shoes. Elastics are used to pull back the matted hair of each into very rough ponytails. Each of them also transfers the contents of their pockets from their old clothes to the new ones.

Once they are changed, they leave again, this time headed for the closest grocery store. The small girl is set inside a shopping cart and watches with wide eyes as they pass through aisle after aisle of food and other items. The petite female is very selective of what she adds to the basket, mainly choosing fruits, vegetables, nuts and breads for food. Some cheap dishes are added, as is a large container of olive oil. A few personal items including hairbrushes finish off the shopping trip. When they reach the check out, the whole lot costs the petite woman nearly all the money she has left. This time everything is packed into bags, which get split between the petite female and the child for the walk back to the basement they are slowly converting into a home.

Inside, the grocery bags are set inside the box which had been used to transport their purchases from the junk shop. Both eat a little bit. Then the petite female picks up the olive oil and a hairbrush.

She has the small girl remove her shirt and settle herself on the floor. The petite female pours a generous amount of the oil onto the girl's hair and works it in well before removing the packaging from the brush. As gently as she can, beginning with the ends, the petite female works the brush through the badly tangled hair. The small girl squirms a little, but remains sitting through the entire process. At the end, once her hair is as smooth as it will ever get, the petite female braids it, securing an elastic around the end of the braid.

The small girl is yawning widely, her eyes glazing over, by the time the petite female is finished. Once she is free to move, she goes over to curl up in one of the newly made beds and is quickly asleep.

Now the petite female works a generous amount of the oil into her own hair and begins the even longer task of detangling it. Eventually, she is able to braid it. As soon as the braid is tied off and the cap is back on the oil, she strips off her clothes, turns off the lantern, and retires to the second bed.

The small girl is still asleep when the petite female gets up and dressed. This time the vest is black denim and laces up, but it is paired with the jeans and shoes from the previous day. Only then does she turn on the lantern, which flickers a little before settling into steady light. In the other bed, the small girl stirs, but does not quite wake. Leaving her be, the petite female helps herself to a bit of cold breakfast.

The child finally wakes, looking disoriented, as the petite female is cleaning up from her meal. The small girl blinks in the lantern light before shrinking back into the blankets. The petite female holds out a piece of fruit, but the child hesitates, wide eyes fixed on the face above the proffered food. Then her growling stomach decides her and she takes the fruit.

While she eats, the petite female surveys the room. After a moment, she shifts around some of the empty crates to form a table and two seats plus some rough shelving. Once those are in place, she unpacks the contents of the box onto the shelving.

When the fruit is gone, the child creeps from her bed, coming over to get more food, which the petite female sets out on the makeshift table. The small girl clambers onto one of the seats and starts into her breakfast. Done organizing their home for the moment, the petite female sits opposite, watching the child eat.

Finally, her stomach more full than at any time in her short life, the girl turns her attention to her companion, studying her critically.

"Who are you?"

The petite female takes a deep breath, her expression turning to a frown, "I..." Her voice is rough from disuse, "I don't..." She coughs to clear her throat, "I don't remember now."

The child frowns, "How can you not remember?" She tilts her head to one side, her eyes still studying the petite female, "Grama once said you'd been around forever. She didn't think you could talk."

The dry chuckle is rough and ends in another cough.

"You don't look very old. Not like Grama."

Again the dry chuckle and cough.

"You don't remember your name at all?"

The petite female shakes her head, "Or my age or where I came here from."

The girl's curious frown deepens, "So what do I call you?"

The response is a shrug, "Pick somethin'."

The child's expression twists indecisively, "I donno."

"What's your name?"

"Brina." She looks around the room, "How d'you know how to do all this?"

The petite female shrugs, "Someone somewhere trained me well, I guess."

"How'd you get so much money yesterday?" Brina slips from her seat and goes to examine the contents of the makeshift shelves, "I never get anythin' that useful."

"You don't pick your marks well."

Brina frowns as she turns back to the seated woman, "Huh?"

"Sure you know how to pick pockets. Most kids here do. But you can't tell a person who'd have money or other valuables from one who doesn't."

The girl's shoulders slump as she turns back to her examination. A moment later, she straightens a little and turns to the petite female again, "Did you do all this for me?"

She shrugs, "It felt necessary."

The words earn her a confused expression, "Felt necessary?"

The petite female just shrugs again.

Brina returns to her seat at the table before asking another question, "Now what?"

"Now..." The petite female studies the child critically for a long moment, "Now you learn to make somethin' of your life."

The girl's frown returns again, "Like what?"

"So long as you're willin' to learn an' try new things, you can become anythin'... anyone... you want to be. Have you ever had a day dream?"

"Kinda," Brina swallows hard, "I wanted me an' Mommy an' Grama to live in a real house an' have good food an' good clothes. Like all the people who walk by an' never see us."

The petite female chuckles, slowly shaking her head, "One lesson at a time, I think. You need to learn to pick your marks."

Brina's shoulders slump, "How's that gonna help?"

"It'll keep us in money so we can eat while you learn the next lesson."

"The next lesson?" The girl looks sceptical.

The petite female chuckles, "One lesson at a time. Let's go." She stands and Brina does the same. Together, they leave their new home, making sure the padlock is secure on the outside of the door.

"Wow!" Brina swallows hard as she watches the petite female count out bills and coins, "That's so much money."

The petite female laughs, pocketing the bills and handing the coins to the girl, "It's less than we spent yesterday."

Brina looks sceptical as she pockets the coins, "Now what? We still have food."

"How 'bout a hot meal?"

The girl nods, her whole face brightening. Then her shoulders slump, "The restaurants never let people like us in."

"We don't look like we did," The petite female reachs for a small hand, "It'll be okay. You'll see."

Hand in hand, they walk to a small diner several blocks from their home. When they enter, the waitress behind the counter barely glances over them. However, once they are seated in a booth, she brings over menus.

"Can I get you something to drink?"

"Water, please." The petite female requests.

"Water." Brina echoes.

"Okay." The waitress hands each of them a menu before going to get glasses of water.

While she is gone, Brina opens the menu. She studies the pictures for a minute before looking up at her companion.

"What is this?"

"It's a menu. It lists all the food the diner serves," The petite female chuckles, "Any idea what you'd like?"

Brina shrugs, "Somethin' hot. I dunno."

The waitress returns to set two glasses on the table and take their order. The petite female orders for both of them and the waitress leaves again.

Brina glances around, seeming somewhat lost in thought before focusing on her companion again, "So what's the next lesson?"

"You learn to read so you can order your own food."

The girl scrunches up her face at the idea, "Learn to read? Just for that?"

The petite female laughs, "Well, not just for that. You'll be amazed what becomes possible when you can read."

Brina appears sceptical, but quits asking questions.

When their food arrives, the girl turns her attention to eating. Or at least until she is full. Then she spends some time studying the petite female across from her.

"You really don't remember your name? At all?"

The petite female takes a deep breath, "I know I've been here a very long time. There was... something... I wanted to forget. But in forgettin' that thing, I seem to 've forgotten a lot of other things."

"Somethin' bad?" Brina shivers.

The petite female shrugs, "Just think of somethin' to call me for now. My memory seems to be slowly comin' back. One day I'll be able to tell you my name."

"I guess," Brina grimaces, "I just... I don't know. You saved me. You aren't family... exactly..."

"Family is what you make it."

The girl frowns, "Huh?"

"Maybe one day you'll understand." The petite female spots the waitress returning with their bill. After a glance at the paper, she hands over a couple bills. The waitress takes them. While she is gone to the till, Brina and her companion leave the diner.

Once they are out on the street, Brina looks up, "So how do I learn to read?"

"We need to buy a few more things." The petite female takes the girl's hand and they start walking, "Paper and pencils would be a good start."

The girl frowns, but seems to withdraw into herself. Just before they reach their destination, she finally brightens and looks up.

"Could I call you Sanah?"

"Sure."

March-63

"Sanah!" Brina is breathing hard and pouring sweat when she dashes inside and slams the door closed. She bolts it securely before leaning against it, "What's the thieves guild?"

The woman across the room looks up from cleaning the knife in her hand, "What happened?"

"I took that job... the one for Reict..." Brina pants, "Any street kid could've done what he wanted an' the pay seemed good..."

Sanah nods, "I thought you would. But what happened?"

"These people came when he was payin' me," Brina slumps down to sit against the door, "Said I shouldn't work for him. Said it was thieves guild territory an' I shouldn't be there. Reict laughed at them. Said they're a useless bunch of nobodies."

"The guild here is a useless bunch," Sanah sets aside the knife, "They've been a joke for years... claimin' to be professional thieves, but can't feed their own any better than anyone off the street."

"So why do this now?" Brina, now breathing easier,

straightens up, "What can they really do?"

"There may be a new local guildmaster," Sanah takes a deep breath, "I've been keepin' an eye on them, but they exist so far underground it's hard to get anythin' accurate."

Brina frowns, "How d'you know so much?"

"Come here," The woman turns so the girl can see her left shoulder clearly, "This tattoo is somethin' given to those who qualify for thieves guild membership, but choose not to join. They like to track potential trouble."

Brina's frown deepens, "How long 've you had it?"

"I wish I knew. What I do know is it's a variation on a guild trainer's crest which hasn't been used in a very long time."

"A variation?"

Sanah shrugs, "I think... any guild trainin' I might've had was secondary to somethin' else. Somethin' more important."

"There was somethin' else..." Brina takes a deep breath, "When the guild people came after me... Somethin' 'bout the infamous Amy. Is that a person? Do you even know?"

Confusion and uncertainty chase each other across the woman's face, "A person... I think. The name's familiar." Finally, she shakes her head, "You did get paid?"

Brina nods, "Reict said he'd send word if he has more work for me. I guess he isn't worried 'bout the guild people."

"I wouldn't worry 'bout them either." Sanah picks up the knife to finish cleaning it.

The girl nods again. A moment later, she queries, "So what's the next lesson? Now that I can pick pockets an' locks an' fight a bit an' read an' write an' do some math."

"Safes," Sanah looks up, "You already have a good eye for value. But learnin' to open safes 'll really increase the jobs you can take."

"Prob'ly." Brina nods to herself.

March-65

As they finish eating their usual cold breakfast, Brina looks at her companion and teacher, "The job I'm s'posed to do today... It'd be a lot easier with two people. The pay's enough to split."

Sanah nods, "Shouldn't be a problem."

The two of them get themselves ready before leaving. As always, they ensure the door is securely locked. Then they set out walking.

Before they have gotten more than a couple blocks, two large men appear on the sidewalk ahead of them. Sanah's eyes turn colder than usual. Brina swallows hard, but keeps up with her companion.

"You shouldn't be here." The man who speaks is just slightly taller than his companion.

Sanah stops just short of them, but does not speak. Brina does the same.

"You shouldn't even be alive," The second man looks contemptuous, "If you're really..."

"You think you know who I am?" The woman shakes her head, "You can't resurrect a dying guild chapter by drivin' others away. If you can't do the work, you won't get the jobs."

The first man draws a gun and the woman explodes into motion, knocking the weapon away and laying out both men before either has opportunity to react. As quickly as she had attacked, the woman is calm and walking again. Brina shivers as she hurries to keep up.

"You really still don't remember how you know how

to do these things?"

The woman takes a deep breath, "I think... I think I was merc trained."

"Merc trained?" Brina frowns, "Like the professional trained mercenaries they tell stories about? There hasn't been a school in decades... longer."

Sanah shrugs, "There's still a lot I don't remember."

"Merc trained and guild trained?" Brina continues to frown, "Who could've gotten both even when the merc schools did exist?"

"Someone who was somethin' more than either."

At the new, female voice, both turn to see a woman with long black hair, blue eyes, and an intricate piece of jewelry dangling from one ear. She is holding an identical piece in one hand.

Sanah frowns in confusion, "I know you."

The black haired woman sighs, "Yeah, you do. But I'm guessin' you did a number on yourself this time."

Brina glances back and forth, looking wary, before addressing the stranger, "Who are you?"

"Most people know me as Lexa Hyrin. I was her trainin' partner... back when we were in trainin'."

"Lexa..." Sanah reaches for the pendant, "This's mine, isn't it?"

Lexa nods, "I had a feelin' you'd need it back. I'm just not sure why you picked now to piss off the thieves guild."

"I didn't set out to," Sanah studies the piece of jewelry before tucking it into a pocket, "We're on our way to a job. Will you be around later?"

"For a day or so," Lexa nods, "Then I have my own job to get to. I'll find you this evenin'."

Sanah nods, "Later then."

When Brina and her instructor return home around sunset, they find Lexa seated on the steps. She stands on hearing them approach. Brina frowns warily.

"How'd you find this place?"

Lexa chuckles, "Wasn't that hard."

Sanah just nods to herself and goes down to let all three into the building basement. Only once the door is closed and locked does she return her attention to their visitor.

"Why look for me now?"

Lexa studies her carefully, "How much d'you remember?"

The other woman sighs, "It's comin' back in bits an' pieces. I know I didn't deliberately block my memory. It was trauma... not that I remember what."

Lexa nods to herself, "How 'bout your name... any or all of it?"

"Amy. Or at least that's what most people call me."

"Well, everyone 'cept your mother an' her best friend," Lexa chuckles, "Most round here 'd prob'ly remember you as Amy Hyrin."

Brina frowns, "Remember her as?"

"Long, long story," Lexa pulls over a crate to sit on, "Has she told you any of what she has remembered?"

"Mostly just stuff related to what she teaches me," Brina gets herself a drink from the ice filled cooler chest beside the shelves holding the kitchen things, "She did say she'd tell me her name once she remembered it. You aren't family..."

"Family is what you make it," Amy sets some food out on the table before pulling up her own seat, "Pretty sure I told you that years ago."

"Somehow I'm not surprised you'd remember that," Lexa looks bemused, "Not sure what else you could call it after this long."

"So you just came to return my pendant?" Amy studies her with a raised eyebrow, "Or is there somethin' else up?"

"Other than you pissin' off the guild? Or at least the local bunch."

Amy grimaces, "Back when I first rescued Brina here, I tried to take her to the local guild. They turned us both away. Said they could barely feed their own, which hasn't actually changed. But there's a new local leader who thinks they can make themselves better again by runnin' any potential 'rivals' out of town."

"So...?"

"So I've been teachin' Brina what I can remember an' we've been takin' odd jobs to get by. Not even necessarily work that could be the guild's jurisdiction, but it doesn't seem to matter. The local guild is fallin' apart faster all the time an' they want to blame everythin' an' everyone but themselves."

"You could just take her out of here."

Amy shakes her head, "Not that simple. Anyway, think you could help me get my pendant back in?"

"Prob'ly." Lexa grimaces.

"Pendant?" Brina frowns, looking from one woman to the other.

"The mark of a trained merc," Lexa explains, "The pendants are given on graduation. And there're very few mercs who'd willingly give theirs up even temporarily."

"I'm not most mercs."

"You're more merc than anything else," Lexa shakes her head, "Always were."

"Long as no one else turns up here."

"Prob'ly the next person who'd come lookin' for you is your husband."

"Husband?" Brina raises an eyebrow.

"He isn't on the continent."

"Yeah, well, you two have very different ways of copin'," Lexa shrugs it off, "Undoubtedly he'll turn up when he's ready."

Brina frowns, "So... wha-...?"

Amy chuckles, turning to her, "I'm not goin' anywhere just yet. You're far from finished your lessons."

"I kinda figured."

"Well, I already told you I'm on my way elsewhere," Lexa reminds them, "You need or want anythin' else, you'll have to get someone else to get it for you."

"I think I've got anythin' I need for now."

April-69

As Amy is walking past the front of the building, she spots a paper tacked to the boards over the door. Going over to investigate, she finds a notice from the city. A frown forms as she reads through the information, deepening rapidly when she realizes the implications. Leaving the paper where it is, she goes around to the basement entrance and lets herself in.

Brina is inside, working on some of her tools, but glances up when Amy enters. On seeing the woman's expression, the teen frowns.

"What happened?"

"That developer's plan was approved," Amy helps herself to a drink from the cooler before sitting, "We have three weeks 'fore they knock the whole area flat."

"Three weeks?" Brina swallows hard, glancing around the basement which has served as their home for eight years, "Where do they expect everyone to go?"

"The people will resettle... find new homes," Amy opens her drink and swallows some of the liquid, "The developer an' city council 're right. This area's an eyesore. There's nothin' left to salvage except the people."

"But it's home to..." Brina breaks off on seeing the woman shake her head, "You've lived here way longer than anyone... longer than anyone's grandparents... how can you not care?"

"Sometimes change is necessary," Amy's eyes meet the teen's, "Sometimes you have to let go an' move on. It isn't about caring or not caring."

Brina blinks, swallowing hard, "Where could we even go? Maybe we don't have much, but to not have a home anymore..."

"We'll have a home," Amy takes a deep breath, "Pack what you need for work or absolutely can't live without."

"Today?"

"We'll go once you're packed."

Brina frowns, "What about you?"

"I have anythin' I'll need."

"So as soon as I've packed my stuff?" Brina shivers, "That's..." She shakes her head, "I don't have a job today, so I might as well pack once I'm done with this." She returns to the task she had been working on.

Amy watches silently, sipping her drink, while the teen finishes her work on her tools.

That done, Brina packs everything away neatly in a hardened leather case. The case is the first thing packed into an ancient old backpack which has been lying around. She adds any other equipment she needs for her jobs and all her clothing. Then she pauses in the middle of the floor, surveying the basement which looks much more like a home than when they had first moved in. Finally, she shakes her head and zips up the backpack.

"All done?" Amy eases herself to her feet.

Brina nods, "Let's just go."

Amy leads the way out of the basement, pausing to padlock the door, before mounting the steps to the street. Brina keeps close, growing increasingly nervous as they walk through the streets. They leave the neighbourhood they have lived in for as long as Brina can remember and cross the city to an area of wider streets and much larger, better cared for homes. Beyond that, they reach a subdivision filled with walled and gated mansions. Brina shrinks close to Amy, who is paying more attention to the street numbers than anything else. Eventually, she stops to open one of the gates and usher Brina onto a property no different from the others around it. Amy follows a narrow stone path to a side entrance into the garage and stretches up, her fingers feeling along a crack beside the door frame. Coming up with a key, she unlocks the door, replaces the key, and ushers Brina into a huge garage containing a single small car.

"What is this place?"

"I'll explain later," Amy leads the teen across the garage and up an inside staircase. At the top, they follow a hallway to the main foyer. An elderly woman appears from one of the rooms on the far side. She studies Amy with widening eyes before shaking her head.

"Ma'am," The elderly woman swallows hard, "Did you just arrive in town?"

"Not exactly," Amy takes a deep breath, "Mrs Gurail?" She waits for the woman to nod before turning to Brina, "This is the housekeeper, Mrs Gurail," Addressing the elderly woman again, she continues, "This is Brina. She'll need rooms... probably for a while."

The elderly woman nods, "Yes, ma'am." She disappears up the stairs.

Brina gazes wide eyed around the foyer before turning to Amy, "You... own... this place."

"It's one of the properties included in the estate my husband controls," Amy leads the girl into the dining room where they can sit until the housekeeper returns, "I haven't been here since Mrs Gurail was newly appointed housekeeper... she was much younger then. But it's a roof over our head the city won't attempt to knock down."

"I guess," Brina swallows hard, "Now what?"

"You finish training," Amy's eyes meet the teen's, "You'll have access to the library here an' I'll be takin' you to a range for firearms trainin'. You're also comin' up on old enough to learn to drive an' if you want to do that, there're people I'll need to talk to 'bout the arrangements."

Brina slowly nods, "I don't have any ID. I'm not sure my birth was even registered."

"There're ways around that," Amy shrugs it off, "Right now, you need some time to settle in here. You're also gonna learn a few things 'bout copin' in polite society."

The teen makes a face, "I'd never pass for anythin' 'cept a street rat."

Amy chuckles, "You'd be surprised what a street rat can be capable of."

Brina studies the woman critically, "Did you really grow up on the street somewhere?"

Amy nods, "Not here," She sighs, "Not anywhere that exists now."

"Your home was destroyed?" Brina shivers.

"The entire town burnt to the ground one summer an' it was decided it wasn't worth rebuildin'."

"A whole town?" The teen looks sceptical.

Amy shrugs it off, "A whole town worse than the neighbourhood we just left. 'Tween that an' the Church, there isn't much out there these days."

"The Church." Brina scowls.

"It is what it is an' it seems to be here to stay a while." Amy does not say anything more because the housekeeper enters the room.

"Ma'am, the master suite is open for you. A suite beside it has been opened for the young lady."

"Thank you." Amy stands, indicating for Brina to accompany her. Leaving the dining room, they go upstairs. At one end of the hallway which runs the width of the house, Amy ushers Brina through an open door.

"Take some time to settle in an' unpack. I need to make a call."

"Okay." Brina swallows hard as she looks around the first room.

Leaving her there, Amy goes down to the telephone in the library. It takes her a moment to remember the number she wants. Once she does, she dials and then listens to it ring and ring and ring. Finally, a breathless female voice answers.

"Hello, Austlan House."

"It's Amy. I need some of my belongings shipped to the house in Settlement City."

"Yes, ma'am. What would you like?"

"My motorcycle an' helmet. My saddlebags, which should have all my tool an' weapon kits in them. My ID an' bank cards. My wedding rings," Amy pauses to think for a moment, "That should be everythin'. Has Malcom been in touch?"

"No, ma'am. To the best of my knowledge, he and Will are at Belstrand. I'll have your belongings shipped as soon as possible."

"Thank you."

"Anything else, ma'am?"

"Not today. I'll call if I need anythin' else."

"Yes, ma'am."

Amy hangs up the receiver, but remains near the telephone for a time before leaving the library and going upstairs to check on Brina.

"So how's this gonna work?" Brina scowls at the papers on the table in front of her, "I don't know any of this."

"Once we get through these, you'll legally be my ward," Amy rolls a pen across the table, "So one blank at a time. You know your first name."

The teen nods and picks up the pen to fill in the first space on the form.

"You'll use my family name since you don't remember any names from your own family. K-R-E-S-S."

Brina frowns, but writes on the third space, "I don't need a middle name, do I?"

"Most people on this continent don't even have one. This form is usually used for immigrants."

The teen looks up at her, "Do you?"

"Amy is my middle name." The woman's expression turns wry. A moment later, she moves on, "Write unknown in the spaces for your parents' names."

"Okay." Brina does as instructed, "What about my birth date? I guess I was born here, but I'm not even sure how old I am. Or do you remember?"

"February, fifteen years ago."

Brina makes a face, "You don't remember the specific day?"

"You were born at a free clinic some time around the middle of the month," Amy shrugs, "Your mother an' grandma were off the street nearly a week."

"So call it the fourteenth," Brina figures, "'Less you think the clinic would have the record."

Amy shakes her head, "That specific clinic burned to the ground years ago. All of their files were lost in the fire."

The teen sighs, "So much for that. What about the rest of this?"

"The rest is for me to fill out an' file. I seriously doubt the CPA 'll contest the request."

"Why would they?" Brina shakes her head, passing the forms and pen across the table, "Most foster kids don't have things this good. But won't they want me in school?"

"You'll be registered as a home schooler," Amy picks up the pen, "Which is nothing more or less than the truth. Maybe you'll never quite be grade twelve equivalent, but what you are learning will serve you better."

Brina nods to herself. "What about your husband?"

"I don't think he'll be returnin' to the continent before you come of age," Amy shrugs it off, "Honestly, even if he did, he wouldn't say anythin'."

The teen takes a deep breath, her eyes going to the woman's face, "Do you remember what happened? Why you're livin' apart? Why you even came here?"

Slowly, Amy shakes her head, "Not so far. But it may be the last thing to come back."

September-72

Amy is in the garage, doing a little bit of work on her motorcycle, when Brina slips in the side door. The young woman comes over to watch the older one work.

Amy glances up, "What happened now?"

"The guild," Brina sighs, "Seems like nothin' can stop this guy."

"The thieves guild has existed since shortly after the Migration," Amy shrugs lightly, "Jailin' a few local leaders isn't gonna make it go away."

The young woman scowls, "Mostly I wish they'd leave me alone. They leave you alone."

"They can't touch a trained merc," Amy sits back on her heels, "Unfortunately that's a protection I can't extend to you."

"So...?"

"You will have your place," The older woman's eyes meet the younger one's, "You've pretty much finished anythin' I can teach you."

"Am I?"

Amy nods, "You prob'ly know more than I did at your age. On the other hand, you're benefittin' from all my years of experience workin' and some improvements in technology over those years."

"You work pretty low tech," Brina grimaces, "Considerin' what's out there."

Amy shrugs, "You may, one day, meet my husband. If you want to talk tech..."

Brina shakes her head, "So how do I stop these guild idiots from harassin' me when I'm workin'? It doesn't seem to matter what kind of jobs I take."

"There's a confrontation comin'," Amy returns to her task, "I'm tryin' to give you everythin' you need to come out on top."

"On top?" Brina raises an eyebrow, "I think I'll settle for survive."

Amy chuckles, "You're gonna have to do better than survive. For now, just keep alert when you're out."

Brina nods, "I need a partner for the job I'm doin' next week. I looked around the area an' there's no way just one person could do what they want."

"Yeah, fine."

On hearing soft movement behind her, Amy turns to see Brina approaching.

"We're done?"

The young woman nods, "We just need to report in." She moves past Amy, who follows her in the direction of their employer's office. They reach the office and get paid without incident, but when they emerge, it is to find several women waiting on the sidewalk. The oldest of them swallows hard on seeing Amy.

Brina scowls, "What now?"

"We need help," The woman takes a deep breath, "If somethin' doesn't change, we're gonna be cut off. We already can't support ourselves."

"So...?" Brina continues to scowl.

"We need a new leader. Someone who actually knows how to be a thief," The woman glances at Amy, "We'd ask you, if it wouldn't get us into more trouble than we're already in."

Amy nods, her expression wry.

"So why me?" Brina is still scowling, "I'm not connected to anything or anyone except her."

"That's why we can ask you," The woman meets her eyes, "Becomin' a guild member is simple. Findin' someone with your trainin' without ties to another organization isn't."

Brina's expression turns sceptical, "What makes you think I'd help you?"

The woman takes a deep breath, "Because he's decided to have you killed. He's plannin' to hire an assassin... maybe already has. He won't quit 'til you stop him because no one else can now."

"I doubt that." The scowl returns.

"You don't want to wait for him to find an assassin who'll take the job," Amy's voice is soft, "End this now,

Brina."

The scowl deepens, "I guess." The young woman sighs, "Where can I find him?"

"You'll have to come with us."

Brina turns to Amy, "You'll come too?"

Amy just nods.

The whole group starts walking, headed towards the building which has housed the local thieves guild chapter since their forced eviction from their previous location. When they get there, they find large thugs guarding all entrances. The woman who had requested Brina's help tries to ignore them and approach the front door, but is stopped.

"No one enters or leaves."

"Since when?" She does not back away.

"Since now." The thug does his best to look intimidating.

Brina's eyes pass over him, "You aren't even a guild member."

"I'm bein' paid to make sure no one enters or leaves." He turns a scowl on her.

There is a flash of silver and he topples over, not quite unconscious, but in too much pain to impede the group. Brina pauses to retrieve the unopened pocket knife she had thrown before accompanying the others inside.

In the main foyer, they find every door closed. The woman who had asked for Brina's help leads the way straight across to a door which turns out to be locked. The others watch, many of them wide eyed, as Brina disarms a clumsily rigged trap and picks the lock. Once the door is open, they enter a dimly lit hall with every door off it closed. The group is led straight to the far end, to another trapped and locked door. Again, Brina disarms the trap and picks the lock.

"He did all this in the time you were gone?" Brina studies the lead woman with a raised eyebrow.

"I think he might've just been waiting for us to leave. Now we really have to be careful. He should be in this next room."

Brina nods. Cautiously, she pushes the door open.

Nothing happens except the women are nearly blinded stepping from the dim hall into the brightly lit room. Brina and Amy blink rapidly until their eyes adjust and they can see the man seated on the far side of the room, surrounded by two rows of the large thugs.

"No one was to enter or leave." The man at the back scowls.

"You would lock people out of their own home?" Brina's voice carries clearly, "You would have someone who's never acted against you killed? You hire outsiders to guard you against your own people? You don't deserve that seat."

"Ain't your business." His scowl blackens.

"Except you keep makin' it my business," Brina shakes her head, "An' I'm gettin' sick of it. You want somethin' done about me, come do it yourself."

"Get them out of here!" His voice spurs the thugs into action.

The first row steps towards the group of women. Brina launches herself forward, easily evading the nearest thugs. She manages to slip through the second row as well, although not quite as neatly. Another step brings her face to face with a drawn gun. Brina ducks faster than he can change his aim, moving around to a position beside his chair. From there, she can see the other women struggling with the thugs. Amy is behind the others, only watching the proceedings. As the gun swings around, Brina catches the man's wrist and wrestles the weapon away from him. She tosses it behind the chair, out of easy reach, then has to dodge a physical attack.

Knowing the man is both larger and stronger than she is, Brina uses all her training in leverage and dirty tricks to subdue him quickly. Soon she has him pinned, the blade of her pocket knife against his throat.

"Call off the thugs."

He scowls, struggling against her and getting the skin of his throat cut in the process, "You won't do anythin' if I don't."

"How deep do you think this blade 'll go?" Brina shakes her head, "Call them off."

"You're nothin' without your teacher."

"My teacher isn't doin' anythin'. Take a look. This's all me an' those who requested my help. Now call them off."

He struggles harder, the knife biting deeper into his throat.

"Call them off while you still have a voice." Brina feels him tensing for another attempt to dislodge her. When he makes no effort to stop the thugs, she uses the butt end of the pocket knife to knock him out.

"No one here's gettin' paid for this." Her voice carries over the sounds of fighting.

"What d'you mean not paid?" The nearest thug turns to face her, then swallows hard on seeing the blood dripping to the floor from the cut in the man's throat, "You killed him?"

"Not killed," Brina shakes her head, "Not yet. Just cut up a little an' out cold. But whatever pay he promised you isn't gonna happen."

The thug frowns, considering her words and eyeing the unconscious man on the floor, "Let's just go," His words are directed to the other thugs, "This's a waste of time." He and those nearest him start for the door. As they get closer, the thugs fighting the guild women disengage and follow. Amy moves aside to allow them to leave. Only once the last of them are out does she move into the room, although just to a place near the door.

The woman who had asked for Brina's help crosses the room to where the young woman is cleaning the blade of her pocket knife on the man's shirt.

"No one here can do anythin' like what you just did," She swallows on seeing the unconscious man, "He isn't...?"

"He's still alive for the moment," Brina eases herself to her feet, "Not that I'd count on anythin' useful from him. Any place we could lock him up for the moment?"

"There..." The woman takes a deep breath, "There're cells, in a level below the basement."

Brina nods to herself, "Is there a way to borrow trainers from other guild chapters? I seriously doubt my trainin' was quite the same."

"Maybe," The woman shrugs, "I don't know what's where right now."

Brina's eyes meet Amy's, "Any ideas?"

"Your trainin' isn't really that far off the guild's usual," Amy tells her, "But this is a mess you'll have to sort without my help."

Brina makes a face, "Do I still have a home?"

"For as long as you need it." Amy chuckles, "I doubt I'll be goin' too far just yet."

The young woman takes a deep breath, "Thanks."

"I'll see you at home." Amy leaves first the room, then the building.

December-77

On hearing the front door, Amy sets her book down. She can hear the housekeeper's hurried steps followed by voices.

"Good afternoon, Miss Kress. Is there anything you need?"

"Just to know where Amy is."

"The library, I believe."

"Thanks."

A moment later, Brina enters the library. After a glance around, she crosses the room to claim the chair beside Amy's. The young woman's eyes go to the book on the arm of the older woman's chair.

"Did you used to read so much?"

Amy nods, "Mainly history an' classical literature, but yeah." Her eyes study the young woman, "What's up?"

"I'm movin' to the Capitol," Brina takes a deep breath, "The continental guildmaster wants me as his apprentice."

Amy raises an eyebrow, "That's an honour."

The young woman nods, "The local guild will actually be in good hands. All most of them needed was a real trainer. Will I see you again?"

"I'm sure you will," Amy smiles, "I'd like you to keep in touch, but I'll be in Wind Valley."

"Wind Valley?" Brina frowns.

Amy nods, "My husband is back on the continent. He's comin' here first, but Wind Valley 's always been his home."

Slowly, Brina nods to herself, "Did you ever remember why?"

The woman sighs, old pain and exhaustion flickering over her face, "Yeah."

Brina glances at the clock on the far wall, "I need to go pack. I'm leavin' by bus this evenin'." She leaves the library.

Amy's eyes go briefly to her book before shifting to

the nearby window.

Amy is standing in the library doorway when Brina comes down, carrying one large bag over her shoulder and another in the opposite hand. The young woman turns almost instinctively to the older one.

"Thank you."

Amy smiles, "You're welcome. Take care of yourself."

Brina nods, "You too. I think my ride to the depot's here. I'll be in touch."

"You better." Amy watches as the young woman goes to the front door to step into her shoes. She remains where she is as Brina leaves the house and the door closes. Outside, a vehicle can be heard pulling away. Almost before the sound fades, another vehicle can be heard pulling into the driveway. That sound is followed by three car doors. Moments later, the front door opens and two men step into the house. Amy crosses the foyer to meet them and is swept into a tight hug. Her arms go around her husband, her face pressing into his chest. After a long moment, the two of them step apart, although only to arms length. Their eyes meet, but neither speaks as they head up to the master suite.

ABOUT THE AUTHORS

Heather Mantler is a lover of fairy tales and fables. She is also a student of psychology. She lives in Prince George, British Columbia and is a member of the writing group Scribblers Unanimous. Heather is always working on another story as she hopes to finish every story idea that she has ever written down. She was a nominee for the fiction category of the 2012 Prince George Regional Arts and Cultural Awards. Heather was short listed for the 2013 John Harris Fiction Awards for this story.

Rosalyn Marie Francis lives in Northern British Columbia. She likes writing, reading, gardening, and spending time with her granddaughter.

A. A. 'Lexa' Cheshire lives in northern British Columbia, Canada. She is a wife and mother who enjoys to read and write fantasy and science fiction.

OTHER WORKS FROM MANTLER PUBLISHING

By B. Heather Mantler

Committed to Her Enemy
Chenarcor

The Kings of Proster Series:
For Wealth and Glory
Closing the Portal
Mistakes Made
Wasted Love
The Mystery of the Magic
The King's Ransom

By A. A. Cheshire

Hunting the Dephlendar
The Price of Devotion
Experiment Redemption Part One
Experiment Redemption Part Two
A Political Marriage
The Keys and the Naph (August 2014)

Beneath the Waves
Kedri Dancer